Band of Brothers

Band of Brothers

Alexander Kent

WILLIAM HEINEMANN : LONDON

Published in the United Kingdom in 2005 by Heinemann Books

1 3 5 7 9 10 8 6 4 2

First published in the United Kingdom in 2005 by William Heinemann

Heinemann Books
The Random House Group Limited
20 Vauxhall Bridge Road, London SW1V 2SA

Random House Australia (Pty) Limited
20 Alfred Street, Milsons Point, Sydney,
New South Wales 2061, Australia

Random House New Zealand Limited
18 Poland Road, Glenfield,
Auckland 10, New Zealand

Random House (Pty) Limited
Endulini, 5a Jubilee Road, Parktown 2193, South Africa

The Random House Group Limited Reg. No. 954009

www.randomhouse.co.uk

A CIP catalogue record for this book is available from the British Library

Papers used by Random House are natural, recyclable products
made from wood grown in sustainable forests. The manufacturing processes
conform to the environmental regulations of the country of origin

ISBN 0 43 401010 3

Typeset by SX Composing DTP, Rayleigh, Essex
Printed and bound in Great Britain by
Clays Limited, St Ives PLC

"The wings of opportunity are fledged
with the feathers of death."
Sir Francis Drake

For you, Boo, with my love.

Contents

1

The Way Ahead

Midshipman Richard Bolitho threw up one hand to shade his eyes, surprised by the fierce, reflected glare from the water alongside. He waited while two seamen lurched past him half carrying, half dragging, some bulky objects wrapped in canvas toward the open deck and the hard sunlight. After the semi-darkness of *Gorgon*'s between decks, it only added to his sense of unreality.

He calmed himself. *Another day.* For most people, anyway.

He glanced down at his uniform, his best. He wanted to smile. The *only* uniform that would pass muster and avoid criticism. He flicked off several strands of oakum which he had collected somewhere along the way from the midshipmen's berth, his home in *Gorgon* for the past year and a half.

Was that really all it was?

He took another deep breath. He was ready; and it was not just another day.

He walked on to the main deck, adjusting his mind to the noise and outward confusion of a ship undergoing the indignities of a badly needed overhaul. Chisels and handsaws, and the constant thud of hammers in the depths of the hull, while elsewhere men swarmed like monkeys high above the decks, repairing the miles of standing and running rigging which gave life to a fighting ship and the sails that drove her. And now it was almost finished. The stench of tar and paint, the heaps of discarded cordage and wood fragments, would soon be a cursed memory. Until the next time.

He gazed across the nearest eighteen-pounders, black muzzles at rest inboard of their ports, still smart, disdaining the disorder around them. And beyond, to the land, hard and sharply etched in the morning light: the rooftops and towers of old Plymouth, with an occasional glitter of glass in the sun. And beyond them the familiar rolling hills, more blue than green at this hour.

He tried not to quicken his pace, to reveal that things were different merely because of this particular day. The new year of 1774 was barely a few days old.

But it *was* different.

Some seamen flaking down halliards glanced at him as he passed. He knew them well enough, but they seemed like strangers. He reached the entry port, where the captain was piped aboard and ashore, and important visitors were greeted with the full ceremonial of a King's ship. Wardroom officers were also permitted here, but not a midshipman, unless on duty in his proper station. Richard Bolitho was not yet eighteen, and he wanted to laugh, to shout, to share it with someone who was free of doubt or of envy.

Out of the blue and with less than a few days warning, the signal had arrived: the appointment every midshipman knew was inevitable. Welcome, dread, even fear: he might receive it with all or none of these emotions. Others would decide his fate. He would be examined and be subject to their decision, and, if successful, he would receive the King's commission, and take the monumental step from midshipman to lieutenant.

He watched a schooner passing half a cable or so abeam, her sails hard in the wind, although the waters of Plymouth Sound were yet unbroken, a deep swell lifting the slender vessel as if it were a toy.

'Ah, here you are, Mr. Bolitho.'

It was Verling, the first lieutenant.

Perhaps he was waiting to board a boat himself, on some mission for the captain; it was unlikely he would be leaving the ship, *his* ship, for any other reason at a time like this. From dawn until sunset he was always in demand, supervising working parties, checking daily, even hourly, progress above and below decks, missing nothing. He was the first lieutenant, and you were never allowed to forget it.

Bolitho touched his hat. 'Aye, sir.' He was ahead of time, and Verling would expect that. He was tall and thin, with a strong, beaky nose which seemed to guide his pitiless eyes straight to any flaw or misdemeanour in the world around him. His world.

But his appearance now was unexpected, and almost unnerving.

Verling had turned his back on the usual handful of watchkeepers who were always close by the entry port: marine sentries in their scarlet coats and white crossbelts, a boatswain's mate with his silver call ready to pipe or pass any command immediately when so ordered. The sideboys, smart in their checkered shirts, nimble enough to leap down and assist any boats coming alongside. And the officer of the watch, who was making a point of studying the gangway log and frowning with concentration, for Verling's benefit no doubt.

Bolitho knew he was being unfair, but could not help it. The lieutenant was new to the ship, and to his rank. He had been a midshipman himself only months ago, but you would never know it from his manner. His name was Egmont, and he was already heartily disliked.

Verling said, 'Remember what I told you. It is not a contest, nor an official corroboration of your general efficiency. The captain's report will have dealt with that. It goes deeper, much deeper.' His eyes moved briefly to Bolitho's face but seemed to cover him completely. 'The Board will decide, and that decision is final.' He almost shrugged. '*This* time, in any case.'

He touched the watch fob that hung from his breeches pocket but did not look at it. He had made his point.

'So you had *not* forgotten, Mr. Dancer. I am glad to know it, sir.'

As if in confirmation, eight bells chimed out from the forecastle belfry.

'Attention on the upper deck! Face aft!'

Calls trilled, and from across the water came the measured blare of a trumpet. Part of life itself. Colours were being hoisted, and there would be several telescopes observing from the shore and the flagship to make certain that no one and no ship was caught unawares.

Midshipman Martyn Dancer exhaled slowly, and nodded to his friend.

'Had to go back to the mess, Dick. Forgot my protector, today of all days!'

It was a small, grotesque carving, more like a demon than a symbol of good fortune, but Dancer was never without it. Bolitho had first seen it after his ordeal with the smugglers. Dancer still bore the bruises, but claimed that his 'protector' had saved him from far worse.

Verling was saying, 'I wish you well. We all do. And remember this, the pair of you. You speak for yourselves, but today you represent *this ship*.' He permitted himself a thin smile. 'Go to it!'

'Boat's alongside, sir!'

Bolitho grinned at his friend. It was only right that they should be together today, after all that had happened.

Lieutenant Montagu Verling watched them climb down to the launch which had hooked on to the 'stairs' beneath the port. Had he ever been like that, he wondered?

'*Cast off! Shove off forrard!*' The boat, caught on the tide, veered away from the big two-decker's side, oars upright in twin lines, the coxswain gripping the tiller-bar, gauging the moment.

Verling was still watching them. It was not like him, and he was a little surprised by it. The carpenter and the boatswain would be waiting with yet more lists, work to be done, stores or cordage not yet arrived or the wrong sort if they had. For he was the first lieutenant. Right aft, beneath that big ensign curling in a steady south-westerly, the captain was in his quarters, secure in the knowledge that this refit would be completed on time. That would please the admiral, and so on, up the chain of command.

Verling saw the oars fanning out on the launch's sides, like wings, while the crew leaned aft to take the strain.

Perhaps, one day soon. . . .

'Give way *together*!'

He swung round, and saw the new lieutenant trying to catch his eye.

It was wrong to harbour personal dislikes in your own wardroom.

He turned and stared across the shark-blue water, but the launch was already out of sight amongst other anchored ships. Suddenly he was glad that he had made a point of being here when the midshipmen had departed, whatever the outcome of their examinations today.

He rearranged his features into the mask of command and strode toward a working party struggling with another tackle-load of timber.

'Take a *turn, you*, Perkins! Jump about, man!'
The first lieutenant had returned.

In spite of the deep swell, the *Gorgon*'s launch soon gathered way once clear of the two-decker's side. Fourteen oars, double-banked, pulling in a strong but unhurried stroke, carried her past other anchored men-of-war with apparent ease. The coxswain, a tough and experienced seaman, was unconcerned. The ship had been so long at anchor during the overhaul that he had grown used to most of the other vessels, and the comings and goings of their boats on the endless errands of the squadron. And the man whose flag flew above the powerful three-decker which he could see in miniature, framed between the shoulders of his two bowmen. The flagship. Like most of his mates, the coxswain had never laid eyes on the admiral. But he was here, a presence, and that was enough.

Bolitho tugged his cocked hat more tightly over his forehead. He was shivering, and tightened his fingers around the thwart, damp and unyielding beneath his buttocks. But it was not the cold, nor the occasional needles of spray drifting aft from the stem. They had all discussed it, of course. Something far away in the future, vaguely unreal. He glanced at his companion. Even that was unreal. What had drawn them to one another in the first place? And after today, would they ever meet again? The navy was like that; a family, some described it. But it was hard on true friendship.

They were the same age, with only a month between

them, and so different. They had joined *Gorgon* together, Martyn Dancer having been transferred from another ship which, in turn, had been going into dock for a complete refit. About sixteen months ago. Before that, he had by his own admission served 'only three months and two days' in His Britannic Majesty's service.

Bolitho considered his own beginnings. He had entered the navy as a midshipman at the tender age of twelve. He thought of Falmouth, of all the portraits, the faces that watched him on the stairs, or by the study. The Bolitho family's might have been a history of the Royal Navy itself.

He thought, too, of his brother Hugh, who had been in temporary command of the revenue cutter *Avenger*. Less than two months ago. He and Martyn had been ordered to join him. An odd and daring experience. He looked over at his friend. That had been unexpected, too. Hugh, his only brother, had been the stranger.

He turned to watch the flagship. Closer now, her reefed topsails and topgallants almost white in the glare, the vice-admiral's flag streaming from the foremast truck like blood. And she had been Martyn's last ship. His only ship. *Three months and two days*. But he was here today for examination. *Like me*. Bolitho had served for five years. There would be others today, bracing themselves, gauging the odds. Did hardened, seasoned officers like Verling ever look back and have doubts?

He stared up at the towering masts, the tracery of black rigging and shrouds. Close to, she was even more impressive. A second-rate of ninety guns with a company of some eight hundred officers, seamen and marines. A world of its own. Bolitho's first ship had been a big three-decker also, and even after some four years aboard in that cramped and busy space there were faces he had never seen twice.

The hull loomed over them, the long bowsprit and jib boom sweeping like a lance. And the figurehead, *Poseidon*, the god of the sea, resplendent in new gilt paint which alone must have cost a month's pay. The 'gilt on the ginger-bread', the sailors called it.

The coxswain called, 'Stand by! *Bows!*'

The two bowmen stood and tapped their blades together to signal the crew to be ready. *A ship shall be judged by her boats.* . . .

There were other boats at the booms or hooked on to the chains. Bolitho saw a lieutenant gesturing to the launch, heard the coxswain mutter, 'I can see *you*, sir!'

Martyn touched his sleeve. 'Here we go, Dick.' Their eyes met. 'We'll show them, eh?'

Like those other times. Not arrogance or conceit. A sort of quiet assurance; he had seen it in the rough and tumble of the midshipmen's berth, and again in the face of real, chilling danger. All in so short a while, and yet they were like brothers.

'Boat yer oars!'

The hull lurched against fenders and the coxswain stood by the tiller-bar again, his hat in one hand. He looked at the two midshipmen. One day they'd be like that bloody

9

lieutenant up there at the nettings, waving his arms about.

But he said, 'Good luck!'

They were on their own.

The officer of the watch checked their names against a well-thumbed list and regarded the newcomers with a cold stare, as if to ensure that they were presentable enough to be allowed further.

He glanced at Dancer's leather crossbelt. 'Take in the slack.' He looked on critically while Dancer tugged the dirk into place and added, 'This is the flagship, so don't you forget it.' He signalled to a young messenger. 'He'll take you to the captain's clerk. Show you where to wait.'

Bolitho said, 'Are there many here for the Board, sir?'

The lieutenant considered it.

'They're not dragging their feet, I'll say that for them.' He relented a little. 'You will be the last today.' He swung round to beckon to another seaman, and Dancer said quietly, 'I hope we can get something to eat while we're waiting!'

Bolitho smiled, and felt sheer hilarity bubbling up. Like a dam breaking. Dancer could do always do it, no matter how tense the situation.

They followed the messenger, the ship reaching around and above them. A teeming world of packed humanity separated only by the invisible boundaries of status or rank. As a mere boy, it had been like being carried on a tide, with all the bumps and bruises, spiritual as well as physical, you might expect along the way. And the characters, the good and the bad, those you trusted on sight, and others on whom you would never turn your back without risk.

And always busy, ceremonial one moment, court martial the next. He felt the smile on his lips again. And always hungry.

The captain's clerk was a pale, solemn individual, who would have passed as a clergyman ashore or in more suitable surroundings. His cabin was close to the marines' messdeck and stores, the 'barracks' as they termed it, and above the other shipboard sounds they could hear the clatter of weapons and military equipment and the thump of heavy boots.

The captain's clerk, Colchester, seemed oblivious to everything but his own work, and the position which set him apart from the crowded world around him.

He waited for the two midshipmen to seat themselves on a bench half-covered by documents neatly tied with blue ribbon. It looked chaotic, but Bolitho had the feeling that Colchester would know immediately if a single item was misplaced.

He regarded them with an expression that might have been patience or boredom.

'The Board today consists of three captains, unlike the more usual practice of one captain and two junior officers.' He cleared his throat, the sound like a gunshot in the paper-filled cabin.

Three captains. Dancer had told him what to expect, to

11

warn him, this very morning, while they had been trying to dress and prepare themselves mentally in the noise and upheaval of the midshipmen's berth. It had seemed worse than usual, and the mess space was further reduced by stores and bedding from the sick quarters nearby.

How had Dancer known about the Board's members?

He did not seem troubled by it, but that was Dancer. His way, his shield. No wonder he had won a kind of respect even from some of the hard men in *Gorgon*'s company.

And from Bolitho's sister Nancy, in the short time Dancer had stayed at the house in Falmouth. She was only sixteen, and it was hard for Bolitho to accept her as a woman. She was more used to the youngsters around Falmouth, farmers' sons, and the callow young men who made up the bulk of the officers at the garrisons in Pendennis and Truro. But it had not been merely his imagination. She and Dancer had seemed to belong together.

Three captains. There was no point in wondering why. A sudden sense of urgency? Unlikely. There were far too many officers in a state of stalemate, with no prospect of promotion. Only war increased demand, and cleared the way on the Navy List.

Or perhaps it was the admiral's idea. . . .

He looked over at Dancer, who appeared serenely oblivious.

Colchester said, 'You will wait here until you are called.' He got slowly to his feet, his lank hair brushing the deckhead beams. 'Be patient, gentlemen. Always fire on the uproll. . . .'

Dancer watched him leave, and said, 'If I get through today, Dick, I shall always owe it to you!'

Not so confident, then. Bolitho looked away, the words lingering in his mind. He had thought it was the other way around.

2

Not A Contest

Waiting was the worst part, more than either of them would
admit. And here they were shut off from life, while the
great ship throbbed and murmured above and around them.
The clerk's cabin consisted merely of the screens which
separated it from the marines' quarters and stores, and was
devoid of ports; the only light came from vents above the
door and two small lanterns. How Colchester coped with
his letters and files was a mystery.

It was now afternoon, and apart from a brief visit by a
young midshipman who had hovered half in and half
outside the screen door as a seaman had delivered a
plate of biscuits and a jug of wine, they had seen nobody.
The midshipman, whom Bolitho thought was about
twelve years old, seemed almost too frightened to
speak, as if he had been ordered not to confide in or

converse with anyone waiting to face the Board.

So young. I must have been like that in Manxman. It had been his first ship.

Even now, *Poseidon* was evoking those memories. Constant movement, like a small town. The click of heels, the thud of bare feet, and the heavier stamp of boots. He cocked his head. The marines must have abandoned their 'barracks' to carry out drills on the upper deck, or some special ceremony. This was the flagship, after all.

Dancer was on his feet again, his face almost pressed against the door.

'I'm beginning to think my father was right, Dick. That I should have followed his advice and stayed on dry land!'

They listened to the rumble of gun trucks, one of the upper deck twelve-pounders being moved. To train a new crew, or for care and maintenance. At least they were *doing* something.

Dancer sighed and sat down again. 'I was just thinking about your sister.' He ran his fingers through his fair hair, a habit Bolitho had come to know and recognise. He was coming to a decision. 'It was such a pleasure to meet her. Nancy . . . I could have talked with her for ages. I was wondering. . . .'

They both turned as the door clicked open. Another seaman this time, but the same midshipman hovering at a distance, the white patches on his uniform very clean and bright in the filtered sunlight from a grating above his head.

'Just come for this gear, sir.' The seaman gathered up the plates and the wine jug, which was empty, although neither of them could recall drinking the contents.

He half turned as the midshipman outside the door answered someone who was passing. Friends, or a matter of duty, it was not clear. But it was like a signal.

He looked quickly at Dancer, then leaned over toward Bolitho.

'I served with Cap'n James Bolitho, sir. In the old *Dunbar*, it was.' He darted another glance at the door, but the voices were continuing as before. He added quietly, ''E were good to me. I said I'd never forget. . . .'

Bolitho waited, afraid to interrupt. This man had served under his father. The *Dunbar* had been James Bolitho's first command. Well before his own time, but as familiar to him as the family portraits. The seaman was not going to ask any favours. He wanted to repay one. And he was afraid, even now.

'My father, yes.' He knew Dancer was listening, but keeping his distance, possibly with disapproval.

'Cap'n Greville.' He leaned closer, and Bolitho could smell the heavy rum. ''E commands the *Odin*.' He reached out as if to touch his arm, but withdrew just as quickly, perhaps regretting what he had begun.

The young midshipman was calling, 'Tomorrow at noon, John. I'll not forget!'

Bolitho said quietly, 'Tell me. You can rest easy.'

The ship named *Odin* was a seventy-four like *Gorgon*, and in the same squadron, and that was all he knew, except

16

that it was important to this seaman who had once served his father.

The plates and the jug clashed together and the man blurted out, 'Greville's bad, right the way through.' He nodded to emphasise it. *'Right through!'*

The door swung slightly and the young voice rapped, 'Come along, Webber, don't take all day!'

The door closed and they were alone again. He might have been a ghost.

Bolitho spread his hands. 'Maybe I was wrong to let him speak like that. Because he knew my father, I suppose. But the rest. . . .'

Dancer made a cautioning gesture.

'It cost him something to come here. He was afraid. More than afraid.' He seemed to be listening. 'One thing I do know. Captain Greville is on the Board, here and now.' He regarded Bolitho steadily, his eyes very blue, like the sky which had begun the day. 'So be warned, my friend.'

The door swung open.

'Follow me, if you please.'

Bolitho walked out of the cabin, trying to remember exactly what the unknown seaman had said.

But he kept hearing his father's voice instead, seeing him. It was the closest they had been for a long, long time.

The young midshipman trotted briskly ahead of them, as if he were afraid they might try to break the silence he had maintained. Perhaps it was policy in the flagship to keep candidates from any contact that might prepare or warn them against what lay in store. It was certainly true that they had seen no other 'young gentlemen' here for the same rendezvous.

Up another ladder and past one of the long messdecks. Scrubbed tables and benches between each pair of guns: home to the men who worked and fought the ship, and the guns were always here from the moment when the pipe called them to lash up and stow their hammocks, to Sunset and pipe down. The constant reminder that this was no safe dwelling but a man-of-war.

Dancer was close behind him, and Bolitho wondered if he remembered these surroundings as intensely after so many months. Like his own first ship, the noise and the smells, men always in close contact, cooking or stale food, damp clothing, damp everything. Most of the hands were at work, but there were still plenty of figures between decks, and he saw a glance here and there, casual or disinterested; it was hard to distinguish in the gloom. The gunports that lined either beam were sealed, a wise precaution against the January chill and the keen air from the Sound; as in *Gorgon*, only the galley fires provided any heat, and they would be kept as low as possible to avoid wasting fuel. The purser would make sure of that.

Another climb now, to the impressive expanse of the quarterdeck, where the day seemed startlingly clear and light. Bolitho stared up at the towering mizzen mast and spars, the furled sails, and the ensign he had seen from the launch this morning, still lifting and curling beyond the poop. About seven hours ago, and the ordeal had not even begun. They had talked about it often enough, been warned what to expect, even if they survived the selection process today. Being successful and actually receiving the coveted commission were often two very different matters. A sign of the times, with promotion only for the lucky, and the clouds of war as yet unknown to those of their own age and service.

A tall lieutenant was standing by the hammock nettings, a telescope trained on the shore, and a boatswain's mate waiting close by. Apart from two seamen polishing the fittings around the compass box and the great double wheel by the poop ladders, the deck was deserted. After the confines of the world below, it seemed an almost sacred place.

Bolitho looked at the land. The hills were edged with copper. Hard to believe it would be dark before long. Perhaps the examination had been postponed. Cancelled.

'So. The last two.' The lieutenant had moved, and sounded impatient. 'You know what to do.' He hardly spared them a glance. 'Get along with you.' He was already striding to the quarterdeck rail, straightening his coat as he went.

Bolitho stared at the fresh gilt paintwork, the scrubbed gratings and perfectly flaked lines and halliards. The empty marines' mess, the sound of oars alongside, no doubt at the ornate entry port. The admiral was about to go ashore, or visit another ship of the line in his command.

Their youthful guide quickened his pace past the wheel, and Bolitho saw that the two seamen were packing away their cleaning gear. Down another hatchway where the deck planking was covered with black-and-white chequered canvas, he could see that the hand ropes were smartly pipeclayed, and a marine sentry, or at least the lower half of one, was standing rigidly beside the screen doors of the great day and dining cabin. The admiral's quarters.

'Wait!' Another screen loomed before them, freshly painted, like white glass in the light from the quarterdeck, similar to the one directly beneath them.

Dancer nudged him with his elbow.

'The admiral's on the prowl. And I thought it was all for *us*!'

He was even smiling.

A servant ushered them into a lobby, partitioned from the main cabin by more screens which could be hoisted and bolted to the deckhead if the ship was cleared for action. There were two or three comfortable chairs sharing the deck space with one of the after battery's twelve-pounders.

The cabin servant studied them severely and pointed to a bench by a sealed port.

'When you are called.' He had the stiff, tired face of a man who had seen it all before. Their midshipman guide had vanished.

They sat, side by side. Almost soundless here, the highest part of the ship. There was a skylight almost directly above them and Bolitho could see the mizzen shrouds and part of a spar, the sky holding its light beyond. After all this time, nearly six years of his life in the navy, and he still had no head for heights. Even now, when the sails cracked and shook and the pipe shrilled *All hands aloft!* he had to force himself to respond.

'When we get back to *Gorgon,* Dick. . . .' Dancer was gazing at the screen door. 'I have something hoarded away for this occasion.'

Nervous now, unsure? It went far deeper. He said lightly, 'You'll be fine, Martyn. *Under full sail*, remember?'

Dancer said in an odd voice, 'You'll never know,' but the smile was back. 'Bless you!'

'Mister Midshipman Dancer?'

They were both on their feet, unconsciously, and the screen door was being held partly open by the cabin servant, as if he were guarding it.

There was no time for words; perhaps there were none to say. They touched hands, like two friends passing in the street, and Bolitho was alone.

He wanted to sit down, to gather his thoughts, perhaps in one of those comfortable chairs, as some act of defiance. Instead, he stood directly beneath the skylight and stared up at the mizzen shrouds and the empty sky, and very slowly, an inch at a time, made his mind and body relax, come to terms with this moment. They had even joked about it. Looked sometimes at the lieutenants and wondered if they had ever had qualms, and, in some cases, how they had passed. And again the face and the words of the seaman kept coming back. He should have stopped him there and then. They were all told often enough never to listen to gossip or condone it. In the crowded world of a man-of-war, it could end in face-to-face confrontation, insubordination, or worse.

He concentrated on the screen door. The great cabin was part of, but so completely separate from, this vast three-decker. Here the captain could entertain his particular friends and favoured subordinates, even the most junior if it suited him. Bolitho himself had been invited into the captain's quarters aboard *Gorgon* on two occasions, once on the King's birthday, when as the youngest present he had been required to give the Loyal Toast, and another to wait upon some female guests, and ensure that they did not stumble on the ladders between decks or entangle their gowns while entering or leaving the boats alongside.

He thought of Dancer again. Always so at ease with women, outwardly anyway. It was not something false, or done for effect; Bolitho had known plenty like that. Martyn Dancer was of a different breed, something he had noticed even when they had first met. His father was a wealthy, worldly man, of influence and authority, who had made it plain from the outset that he was opposed to his son's choice of career. *Throwing his wits to the wind*, as he had put it more than once.

And he had seen it in his sister's eyes when she and Martyn had talked and laughed together. And in the watchful glances from his mother.

He walked to the opposite end of the screened lobby and peered through to the big double wheel, at the scrubbed gratings where two or more helmsmen would stand when the ship was under way, and heeling over to her towering pyramid of canvas. Another grating was propped upright by the mizzen, probably to dry, but suddenly reminiscent of those far-off days in *Manxman* and the first flogging he had ever witnessed. It was something you had to accept, a necessary discipline. What else would deter the persistent offender?

Accept, perhaps, but Bolitho had never grown accustomed to it. And yet he had seen some of the older hands bare their backs and boast of their endurance of the cat, as if the terrible scars were something to be carried with pride.

He could still remember standing with the other midshipmen, the very first time he had heard the pipe, 'All hands lay aft to witness punishment!'

He had found himself gripping the arm of another middy, his entire body shaking to every crack of the lash across the torn skin.

And that other stark and brutal memory, which never completely left him, months or even a year after that, when he had been face-to-face with an enemy, unskilled and desperate, and carried bodily by the stamping, cursing crush of boarders across the other vessel's deck. Pirates, smugglers, rebels . . . they were the enemy. Cutlass, pike and boarding axe, their faces masks of hate and anger. Sailors he knew, or thought he knew, stabbing and hacking heedless of the screams, men falling, voices urging them forward.

And then there had been one face, so near that he could smell the sweat and feel his breath, and eyes which had seemed to fill it. He remembered seeing the blade, like a cutlass, and had wanted to cry out; he had been gripping the hanger in his fist as if he were holding on to life itself. The blow to his shoulder had numbed it before the agony began. But the eyes were still staring at him, fixed with shock or disbelief. And then he fell, the weight of his body almost dragging the blade from Bolitho's fingers.

And a harsh voice almost in his ear; he had never discovered whose. 'Leave 'im! 'E's done for!'

Done for. He had killed someone. A lifetime ago.

He could still feel the blade jerk in his fist, as if he had only just been called to action, and seen a human being fall beneath his stroke.

He swung round and found the cabin servant watching him. No sound, no word; he had even lost track of time.

'Come, sir.'

It was too soon. Where was Martyn? But the door to the inner cabin was open. Waiting.

He thought suddenly, wildly, of Lieutenant Verling's words this morning.

It is not a contest.

He strode past the servant and heard the screen door close behind him.

Two tables had been placed end to end across the big dining cabin, behind which sat the three captains of the Board. It was like walking onto a stage with no audience, only the three motionless figures who were framed against the flag captain's private day cabin behind them. The stern and quarter windows held and reflected every sort of light, from the sea below and beyond the poop, to the deepening purple haze of the main anchorage. There were already candles burning, so that the three figures on the other side of the table were almost in shadow.

There was one tall chair facing them. If any uncertainty still lingered in the newcomer's mind, it was quickly dispelled: a sword, complete with belt, was laid across it.

Bolitho stood beside it, and said, 'Richard Bolitho, midshipman, sir!' Even his voice sounded unfamiliar.

He thought fleetingly of Dancer. How had he fared at this table? All it needed was the sword lying across it with the point toward him, and it would be more like a court-martial than an interview that might lead to promotion.

'Be at your ease, Mr. Bolitho. You are here today because others are prepared to recommend you. Be truthful and frank with us, and my brother officers and I will be likewise.'

Captain Sir William Proby did not trouble to introduce himself; there was no need. An unorthodox, some said eccentric, officer who had distinguished himself in the Seven Years' War and in two campaigns in the Caribbean, he had served until recently as acting-commodore with the Channel Fleet. It was rumoured that he was next in line for flag rank.

Bolitho had seen him several times when carrying despatches to his present command, the *Scylla*, a seventy-four like *Gorgon*, but half her age.

The officer sitting on his right he also knew. Captain

Robert Maude was comparatively young, with an alert, intelligent face, and he commanded the *Condor*, a sleek thirty-two gun frigate, and was doubtless envied by many because of it. *Condor* was rarely at anchor for long; even now Maude was glancing through the adjoining cabin, perhaps at the shadows on the water, or the small boat passing the flagship's quarter and showing a solitary lantern.

The third member of the Board sat with one elbow on the table, his free hand resting on some certificates. And a midshipman's log.

My log.

Even if he had never met or spoken with the unknown seaman, he felt he would have recognised Captain John Greville of the *Odin*. He could still hear the voice. *Greville's bad. Right the way through.*

A narrow, pointed face, not unlike that of Verling, but tight-lipped, very contained. The eyes were in shadow.

Proby said, 'In matters of general seamanship your reports read well. It seems you suffer from an acute dislike of heights, but you have overcome it.' A hint of a smile. 'Outwardly, at least. Having taken charge of a landing party with ship's boats, what cover would you prepare if resistance was expected?'

'Round shot, if a gun was available, sir. To give time for my people to move into position.'

Proby opened his mouth as if to answer, and frowned as Captain Greville said sharply, 'Grape or canister would be far more effective, I would have thought.'

'Later, perhaps, sir. But there is too much risk with either of hitting my own men.'

Greville ruffled the corners of the papers. 'A few eggs have to be broken sometimes, Bolitho!'

Proby tapped the table.

'They are *people*, John, not eggs.' But he was smiling as he turned to his other side. 'You have some points on gunnery, Maude? While we touch upon the subject.' Polite, but strangers.

Maude leaned forward, and Bolitho guessed that he was very tall. It would be a constant handicap below decks in a frigate.

'In a large ship of the line, a three-decker,' he lifted his hand, 'this one, for instance. The order to beat to quarters has just been called, and the ship cleared for action. You are stationed on the lower gun deck and in charge of a division. What precautions will you take?' The hand gestured again. 'Consider it.' He was leaning back in his chair now, his head slightly on one side, as if completely relaxed, and Bolitho felt his own tension slipping away in response. Maude's voice, or perhaps his manner, seemed to exclude the others, and ease his uncertainty. It was almost like having a conversation with an old friend.

He said, 'Lower gun deck, thirty-two pounders, "Long Nines".' The hand moved very slightly, and he went on, 'Nine feet long, sir.' He saw him nod, as if to encourage him. 'Seven men in each gun crew, the captain responsible for giving a set task to each one and assigning a number to each. The lower the number, the greater the skill.'

Proby cleared his throat loudly. 'Suppose this ship is about to engage an enemy to wind'rd? With the deck tilting to the wind, how would seven men manage to haul the gun up to its port? A "Long Nine" weighs a pretty piece, I'd say.'

Bolitho wanted to lick his dry lips. Anything. He answered, 'Three tons, sir.' He waited, but nobody commented. 'I would take men from the gun on the opposite side. With the same precautions to ensure no hands and feet were broken or damaged when the gun recoiled. But bandages should always be close by.'

'You seem to care a great deal for their welfare, Bolitho. But the fight should always come first.'

Bolitho felt his fingers relax. He had not realised that his hands had been so tightly clenched. It was Greville. In some strange way, the challenge was almost a relief.

He said, 'Badly injured men cannot fight a gun, sir. It could delay a complete broadside.'

'But the battle is joined.' It was Maude again. 'Loading, firing, and once more running out. Provided, of course, that *you have enough men.* Is there anything else against which you should guard?'

'Every third shot or so, I'll have the barrel cleaned out, its full length, with the worm and then the sponge. Remove any burning fragment. And to prevent a misfire when a new charge is rammed home.'

Maude nodded. 'Discipline is everything in gunnery, as in most matters in our service. *All orders will be obeyed without question* – I daresay you have heard that a few hundred times since you donned the King's coat?'

Bolitho looked at him. A strong, proud face, not unlike the sketches of Captain James Cook he had seen in the *Gazette*, accompanying tales of his latest voyages. A man you would willingly serve no matter what.

He said, 'It is far easier to drive than to lead, sir. But I believe that trust is all important. On both sides.'

Maude folded his arms.

'Only then will you get the dedication you need when the odds are against you.'

Proby glanced past him. 'Is that all, Maude?' and swung round abruptly on his chair. 'What the *hell*! I gave strict orders!'

But all three captains were on their feet, and the air was suddenly sharp, blowing from the outside world. The creaking of the rigging was audible now, and the occasional scream of gulls circling over incoming fishermen.

Bolitho wanted to turn and identify the newcomer, who had burst uninvited and unexpectedly into this meeting.

Like waking from a bad dream, he thought, a nightmare: the three captains rigid behind the table, and Maude's height indeed compelling him to bend beneath the deckhead beams.

'Excuse my untimely interruption, gentlemen. My barge is alongside, and I would not wish to keep my cox'n waiting much longer. But I wanted to bid you farewell, and thank you for carrying out these duties, from which we shall all benefit in due course.'

Bolitho flinched as a hand touched his sleeve.

'And who is this? I was assured that you had finished here today.' It sounded more like an accusation than an apology.

Bolitho turned and faced him. He had seen him only once before, when his own boat had tossed oars to the barge and he had had the briefest glimpse of Vice-Admiral Sir James Hamilton, the great man himself. His uniform and lace gleaming in the reflected light, cocked hat casually balanced in his other hand. Half smiling now.

'Cornishman, eh?'

He knew his mouth had moved and he had said something, but it had been like hearing someone else blurting out his name.

The admiral was looking keenly at him. It felt like being stripped.

Then he nodded, as if some thought had dropped into place, some inner reference been made.

'I hope the future is kind to you, er, Bolitho.' He turned away, the contact broken. 'Now I must leave you. I have duties ashore. Events are moving once more.' He reached the door and Bolitho could see the flag captain hovering, with a boat cloak draped carefully across his arm.

For a long time, or so it seemed, they all stood in silence, swaying only occasionally as the flagship pulled at her cable.

Bolitho realised that Sir William Proby was seated once again, his expression a mixture of bemusement and relief.

'An unforeseen interruption, gentlemen.' He paused to

listen as calls trilled in the distance, followed by the muffled bark of commands. The admiral's barge was casting off.

'If you have no further questions?' He was not, apparently, anticipating any. He looked at Bolitho. 'Be seated, if you please.'

Bolitho stared at the solitary chair. The sword had vanished.

Proby scratched his quill across a certificate, and said, 'On behalf of this Board, Mr. Bolitho, I congratulate you.' He came around the table before Bolitho could lever himself out of the chair. Proby was a substantial figure, but he had scarcely seen him move.

He was on his feet finally and Proby was shaking his hand and saying, 'We wish you a speedy promotion!' Now it was Maude's turn, shaking his hand abruptly and looking down at him, with a smile he would always remember. He had passed. It might be next month, or a year from now, before he actually received that lieutenant's commission. *But he had passed.* The cabin servant was placing some fine goblets on a tray. But there were only three. He took a deep, deep breath, wanting to laugh, or cry.

It was over. And it was dark beyond the stern windows. He picked up his hat and walked to the door, almost expecting his legs to fail him. *It was over.* He must find Martyn, make sure that. . . . He paused and glanced back at the cabin, the hands reaching for filled glasses. Tomorrow they would have forgotten him, put it behind them. It was only another examination.

Captain Greville had not shaken his hand. And he was glad of it.

He saw the bench where they had waited. No turning back. No matter what.

I am a King's officer. Almost. Then he did touch his eyes.

3

A Favour for the Captain

Lieutenant Montagu Verling stood at *Gorgon*'s quarter-deck rail, his hands on his hips, watching a party of seamen clambering over the boat-tier below him. One of the ship's two cutters swayed across the nettings like an ungainly whale, while Hoggett, the boatswain, gestured with his fist, his voice carrying easily above the noise of other work and the clatter of loose rigging.

'This will not take long.' Verling swore softly as a seaman slithered and fell on the wet planking. It had been raining all night, and now in the grey forenoon the weather showed little improvement. Plymouth was almost hidden in mist, a spire or rooftop showing here and there like projections of a reef.

Bolitho was also watching the cutter, now being moved into position above the tier. At last they were replacing things, and most of the debris left by the refit had vanished. Some lashings remained to be done, and canvas awnings had been spread to protect paintwork and fresh pitch. Between decks, order had already been restored, with stores and spare equipment stowed away, and messdecks cleared of clutter and gear that belonged elsewhere in the hull.

He tried to stifle a yawn, surprised that he had been able to drag himself out of sleep and present himself on deck at the chime of the bell. He turned to peer above the quarterdeck nettings with their neatly stacked hammocks, the cold air wet on his face. Even that did not revive him, and there was a painful crick in his neck. He saw the topmasts of the big three-decker drifting out of the mist at the far end of the anchorage. The flagship; he could even make out the vague dash of colour from her ensign. The bulk of the ship remained hidden by the fog. He winced, but his spirits soared at the memory. Had that been only yesterday? Was it possible?

'Lower away, 'andsomely there!' Hoggett's voice, which seemed even louder on this raw morning.

The cutter began to descend, the men on the tackles taking the strain, feet somehow finding a grip on the slippery planking.

''Vast lowering!'

He heard Dancer give a groan.

'My *head*, Dick. I feel like death!'

Even the Board itself was hard to fix in the mind, like a dream fast disappearing. Only certain moments remained clear: the three figures at the table. An empty chair. And the sudden, startling interruption when the admiral had made his entrance. Perhaps the handshakes remained most vivid in his memory. *We wish you a speedy promotion!*

Then back to *Gorgon*, in darkness, passing an over-loaded boat full of sailors, all of whom sounded drunk, probably just paid off from some merchantman. He and Dancer had been unable to stop laughing at the string of curses launched by their own coxswain. Then, in the midshipmen's berth, the heavy silence of some, hunched over written notes, studying or pretending to, by the flickering light of glims, or apparently asleep, being shattered as they had risen as one: a midshipman's salute to any successful candidate for promotion. Hoarded drinks appearing, which had ranged from blackstrap to cognac, helped down by beer from the mess cask, with a mock fight known as 'Boarders Away!' to round off the occasion. It had taken threats of physical violence from the warrant officers' mess to quieten the celebration.

Bolitho cleared his throat, or tried to. And now the captain wanted them aft, in the great cabin.

Verling waved to the boatswain as the cutter finally came to rest on the tier. Even the new paint was unmarked.

He said, 'The Captain is going over to *Poseidon* very soon. The admiral has called a conference – all senior captains. Something's in the wind.' He gazed critically at the two midshipmen. 'Under the circumstances, I suppose. . . .' He left the rest unsaid.

Bolitho thought of the admiral again, the hand on his arm. *I have duties to perform. Events are moving once more*. Was that the real reason he had interrupted the examination?

Without it, what might have happened? He recalled Greville's sarcasm, his refusal to shake his hand.

He had mentioned it to Dancer, and he had passed it off by saying, 'Greville shook *my* hand, but I could have done without it! I still can't remember half of what I said to them. I was in a daze!' It was something shared after that, real. They had hugged one another, each glad for the other.

And now they were to see the captain. After all this time, he remained remote, almost unknown. And yet nothing had any real purpose without him, without his presence. At any ceremonial, or drill with sails and guns, he was always there, usually with Verling nearby, an extension of himself. He was there to announce any achievement by the ship, or even an individual, and to read the Articles of War before awarding punishment.

Bolitho had once heard a friend of his father's say that when a King's ship was away from the fleet, and free of the admiral's apron strings, all that stood between a captain and chaos were the Articles of War and a line of marines across the poop. And he still recalled his father's quick retort. *'It would all depend on that captain!'*

Only yesterday . . . and yet he could feel the change in himself, sense the scrutiny of the younger midshipmen. As if he represented something, some possibility no longer beyond their grasp. *How does it feel to be one of them?* He was still grappling with his own emotions, and the prospect of a new future.

Verling had tugged out his watch.

'I shall take you aft.' He faced them again. 'Several others failed to satisfy the Almighty yesterday.' He did not smile. 'Not certain what *I* would have decided!'

They followed him aft, not quite reassured.

Captain Beves Conway was standing by a small desk fastening the cuff of his shirt. His dress uniform coat hung across the back of a chair, with his hat nearby. He was preparing for the admiral.

They had passed *Gorgon*'s surgeon as he was leaving, a stooping figure of indeterminate age, with a thin, almost lipless mouth. Bolitho had heard some of the old Jacks say that he would rather bury you than cure you if you ever fell into his hands, but they said that about most surgeons. He wondered what he had been doing for the captain. He had noticed that Conway sometimes held one shoulder stiffly, like now, as he slipped into his coat. A wound he had taken during the Caribbean campaign against the French, he had heard, although others had hinted at a duel fought, of course, over a lady.

He realised that there was another person in the cabin, perched on a chest by the screen, the captain's coxswain. A big, powerful man, always smart and instantly recognisable in his gilt-buttoned coat and nankeen breeches, he seemed to come and go as he chose. More like a trusted companion than a subordinate.

He was holding a drawn sword now, running a cloth slowly up and down the blade. He glanced briefly at the two midshipmen, but nothing more. He belonged. They were merely visitors.

Conway smiled.

'You did well, both of you. Full credit to the ship also.'

Verling said, 'I'll come aft when you're ready, sir.'

The screen door closed behind him. He had spoken to the marine sentry by name when they had arrived at the lobby. A gift, or careful training? It was impossible to know, but Bolitho guessed it was rare enough. He had known some officers who had never cared to learn a name and match it to a face.

He had heard Verling quietly rebuking one of the senior midshipmen, who had since gone to another ship. 'They are people, flesh and blood. Remember that, will you?'

Bolitho wondered if he had passed or failed at his Board.

The captain said suddenly, 'A moment,' and beckoned. 'Come and see *Condor* spread her skirts – a sight that never fails to excite any true sailor!'

They followed him into the main cabin where the stern windows reached from quarter to quarter, and the panorama of ships and anchorage shimmered against the salt-smeared glass like some unfinished painting.

And here was the frigate *Condor*, topsails and fore-courses already set and filling to the wind now shredding the sea mist, her masthead pendant and ensign stiff and bright as metal against the clouds.

Yesterday. Her captain twisting round in his chair aboard the flagship, gauging the sea, the mood of the weather. Impatient to go. And no wonder.

He turned as Conway asked, 'Do you see yourself in command of a frigate one day, Bolitho?'

'Given the chance, sir. . . .' He got no further.

Conway moved closer, watching *Condor*'s, outline shorten, her yards shifting as she changed tack toward open water and the sea. He said, 'Don't wait to be given the chance. Take it. Or others will.'

He turned abruptly and walked across the cabin. Bolitho wanted to hold the moment, cherish it. This was *the captain*, as he might never see him again. Perhaps older than he had thought, but virile and vigorous, something the streaks of grey at his temples and the crows' feet around his eyes could not flaw or diminish.

He said, 'This damned overhaul is all but finished, thank God.' He looked up and around the cabin, perhaps without seeing it, or seeing it in a way they could not yet understand. 'This lady will be fit and ready for sea again if I – and the first lieutenant – have any say in the matter. After that –' He touched the chair that stood squarely facing the constantly changing panorama. 'Who can say?'

His expression changed and seemed angry, embarrassed. He said almost sharply, 'I have a favour to ask. I've taken enough of your time and the ship's as it is.'

Bolitho saw Dancer gripping a fold of his coat, another habit he had come to recognise, and sometimes understand. It happened when he was surprised, or moved, by something he had not anticipated.

Captain Beves Conway, experienced post captain, who

had seen action and served in most waters where the ensign commanded respect, had a favour to ask?

Beyond these massive timbers, the other world continued to function unimpaired. The trill of a boatswain's call and a shouted command, too muffled to distinguish. The squeal of tackles as another load of stores or equipment was hoisted aboard. A ship preparing for sea. It was what Conway cared about most. Perhaps all he cared about.

He said, 'You will be leaving *Gorgon* shortly on a brief passage duty.' There was a suggestion of a smile. 'Not like your daring adventure with the revenue service, Bolitho. I believe your own brother was in command on that occasion. A family affair, it would seem.' The smile was gone. 'But it will stand you in good stead when you are finally commissioned. Mr. Verling will give you the details.'

It was like a fist striking out of nowhere.

Conway was leaving the ship. Giving up command. And it was all he had.

'A new midshipman is joining tomorrow forenoon. His name is Andrew Sewell, and he is fifteen years old.' He glanced from one to the other, suddenly relaxed, as if some weight had been lifted from him. 'A mere boy compared with you seasoned mariners. He has everything to learn, and it was his father's dearest wish that he should follow his family's tradition and become a sea officer. His father was a great friend of mine, perhaps my best, but, alas, now dead . . . Just offer him a hand when it is needed. Will you do that?' Like a challenge. 'For *me*?'

Bolitho turned as Dancer asked, 'First ship, sir?'

'Not his first.' Conway looked at the reflections rippling across the curved deckhead. 'He has served for two months in *Odin*, Captain Greville, and before that in the *Ramillies*, with the Downs Squadron.'

He looked from one to the other. 'I know, from your behaviour and your reports, and what I have seen for myself, that you are well suited to your profession. Maybe because you come from very different backgrounds, or in spite of it. It might be said that young Andrew Sewell is totally unsuited, a victim of circumstances.' He shrugged, and Bolitho saw the flicker of pain in his face.

The marine sentry stamped his feet, somewhere beyond the screen. Verling must be back, and was waiting.

Conway said, 'My old friend is dead. It is the last thing I can do for him, and perhaps the least.'

His coxswain had appeared, his hat beneath his arm, and Conway's sword in his fist. No words: like an understanding between them.

Dancer offered, 'My father was firmly against my going to sea, sir.'

Bolitho nodded. 'And I never had any choice, sir.'

Conway held out his arms as his coxswain deftly clipped the sword into place.

'So be it, and I thank you. Young Andrew must learn that you do not necessarily have to leave your own deck to confront an enemy.' He shook hands gravely with both of them. 'May good fortune go with you.'

He half turned, as if unwilling to leave. His coxswain had

already departed, and Verling's shadow stood across the outer screen.

'When you return to the ship your new orders may be waiting for you. If not, then be patient.' He picked up his hat and visibly squared his shoulders. He was in command again.

The two midshipmen waited without speaking, listening to the shouted commands and, eventually, the calls as the side was piped and Conway's gig pulled away. Then Dancer murmured, 'Whatever ship I join, I'll never forget *him.*'

They left the great cabin in silence, passing the same marine sentry, their weariness, headaches and sore throats forgotten.

Bolitho considered the passage duty Conway had mentioned. Probably helping to move another ship to different moorings, for some refit or overhaul. And after that . . . He glanced over at Dancer. They would be parted. It was the way of the navy.

Like Conway. Saying goodbye; the hardest duty of all.

4

Hotspur

Martyn Dancer gripped the launch's gunwale and pointed across the larboard bow.

'There she is, Dick! The *Hotspur*! I'll not want to leave this beauty when the time comes!'

Excitement, or sheer pleasure: Bolitho had not seen him like this before. Perhaps strain and uncertainty, which he had always been able to conceal, were at last giving way.

Bolitho felt it, too. The *Hotspur*, which had not even been discussed until today, as if it were a sworn secret, was a topsail schooner, small if set against any frigate or brig; but her style and lines would catch any real sailor's eye immediately.

She was lying at her anchor, and rolling evenly in the swell, showing her copper, bright in the forenoon sun, and the rake of her twin masts. A thoroughbred, and said to be new and untried, straight from her builder.

But the ensign flying from her gaff and the few uniforms moving about her deck were identical to those they had left astern in *Gorgon*, and all the other men-of-war that lay at Plymouth. She was a King's ship.

It was difficult to accept the speed of the events which had brought them here. From the moment they had reported to the first lieutenant, their feet had barely stopped. Until now.

Verling had explained, almost curtly. They were to be part of a passage crew, not to move some hulk or ship awaiting overhaul, but to deliver *Hotspur* to the authorities in Guernsey, as a replacement for an older vessel used in the waters around the Channel Islands for patrol and pilotage. It was another world to them.

And an escape, after all the waiting and doubt, and then yesterday's climax. Again he felt the exhilaration run through him, like his friend beside him. Dancer was pointing at the schooner again, calling something to the cutter's coxswain. And it was the same coxswain and boat's crew which had taken them to the flagship. He heard Dancer laugh and nudged him sharply with his elbow. This sense of light-hearted freedom and excitement would cut no ice with Verling, who was sitting silent and straight-backed by the tiller. The first lieutenant was always very strict when it came to behaviour in boats, maintaining that the ship would be judged accordingly, as every middy soon learned when he came under that disapproving eye.

But even Verling seemed different. It was something in the air, from the start of the day when the hands had been called to lash up and stow their hammocks.

Bolitho had seen the captain speaking with him just before the cutter had cast off. Maybe it was only imagination, but Conway, too, seemed altered, unlike that brief interlude in the great cabin; the mood of defeat, almost valediction, had vanished, and the old Conway had returned. Bolitho had seen him clap Verling on the shoulder this morning, had even heard him laugh.

There were rumours, of course. In a hull crammed with some six hundred sailors and marines, there were always those. But this time there was substance; the reason for the captains' conference, they said. More trouble in the colonies, particularly in Boston, Massachusetts. Unrest fuelled by increased taxes and repressive legislation from London had taken a more aggressive form, too often clashing with the local administration and so, eventually, the military. Although the British were hardened to war and the threat of rebellion, the infamous memory of what had come to be called the Boston Massacre had left a far deeper scar on the public conscience than might have been expected; a radical press had made certain of that. Bolitho had still been serving in *Manxman* when it had happened, and remembered poring over accounts in the news-sheets. A crowd of young people disturbing the peace on a winter's night and coming face-to-face with soldiers from the local garrison, common enough here in England, but more incendiary in a colony chafing under what it believed to be unjust taxation, and seeking a louder voice in its own affairs. At a different time, perhaps a different man might have diffused the situation, but the officer who was present had been convinced that only a show of force would disperse the crowd, and the resulting volley of shots had killed half a dozen of the troublemakers. It was hardly a massacre, but it was bloodshed, and the echoes of those muskets had never since been allowed to fade.

But to those who lived and all too often died on the sea, it meant something else: the need for readiness. Ships to be brought out of dock and stagnation, men to be found to crew, and, if required, fight them. And perhaps officers of merit and experience, captains like Conway, would view any unrest in America as a fresh chance of personal survival. Bolitho had heard his own brother Hugh say as much during their time together in the revenue cutter *Avenger*. Just weeks ago, and it already seemed like an eternity.

His brother had been reserved, almost unknowable, and not only because he had been in temporary command. He looked over at Dancer. It was strange; he had heard Hugh speaking earnestly and intently to him on several occasions when they had been on watch together. Two people who could have so little in common. And yet. . . .

'They've seen us at last! Thought they'd bin so long at anchor they'd forgot what they joined for!'

That was the cutter's other passenger, 'Tinker' Thorne, *Gorgon*'s senior boatswain's mate. There was no yarn that might be spun around him that could not be true. It was impossible to guess his age, although Bolitho had heard that Tinker had served in one ship or another for twenty-five years. Originally from Dublin, a Patlander, as all Irishmen were nicknamed by the lower deck, it was said he came of gypsy stock, and had begun life mending pots and selling fishing gear on the roads. He was not tall, but stocky and muscular, with skin like old leather and fists that could handle any unruly hawser or argumentative seaman before you could guess the next move. He was watching the *Hotspur*, her tapering masts rising now above the double-banked oars, his expression amused and a little critical. His eyes were bright blue, like those of a much younger man looking out from a mask. Admired, respected, or hated, 'It's up to you, boyo,' as he was heard to say when the occasion arose.

He shifted around on the thwart and said, 'Let some other Jack take the strain while we're away, eh, sir?'

Nobody else in the ship could speak so offhandedly to Verling.

Verling was still looking astern. His face was hidden, but his thoughts were clear enough.

'I hope so, Tinker. If we've forgotten anything. . . .'

'Ah, even the cook knows what to do, sir.'

Bolitho watched them with interest. It was important that *Hotspur* was in safe hands until she was delivered to her destination; and Verling had despatches with him, from Conway and probably the admiral. It seemed significant, and would do Verling's own chances of promotion no harm.

But every pull of the oars was taking Verling away from the ship, and the life he cared about most, and like Bolitho's brother Hugh, he had become unfamiliar. It was like meeting a stranger.

He returned his attention to the schooner, larger and heavier than he had first thought, but with a grace any true sailor would relish.

Tinker Thorne saw his eyes, and grinned.

'Old John Barstow is the finest builder in the West Country, that he is. A strange one an' no mistake, swears to God he's only once sailed out of sight of land, an' that was when he was caught in a fog off the Lizard, if you can swallow that!'

The coxswain brought the cutter smoothly alongside, with oars tossed and a bowman ready with his boat hook.

Verling seized the ladder and said, 'You can carry on, 'Swain. Watch those tackles when you stow the boat on the tier. It's all new. Untried.'

'Aye, sir. I'll keep a weather eye on things.'

He might have been mistaken, but Bolitho thought he and Tinker winked at one another. But Verling was turning to look once more at *Gorgon*.

A small side party had assembled on the schooner's deck, and a net was rigged to hoist any personal gear on board.

They waited for Verling, as senior in the boat, to leave first, and Dancer murmured, 'Look who's here, Dick. Surely he's not coming with us?'

It was Egmont, the newest and most junior in *Gorgon*'s

wardroom. He raised his hat in salute as Verling climbed over the gunwale, while the side party came stiffly to attention, or tried to. The schooner was no two-decker and the seamen were more used to *Gorgon*'s massive bulk than a hull that seemed alive in the offshore current. Egmont almost lost his balance, but managed to blurt out, 'Welcome aboard, sir!'

Verling returned his salute coolly and paused to look forward along the deck. Bolitho could not see his face, but guessed he was missing nothing, not even the young lieutenant's discomfort and anger. And, he saw, he had no difficulty in keeping his balance.

Verling said, 'I trust everything is in hand, Mr. Egmont. I see that the boats are stowed, so nobody is still ashore?'

Egmont straightened his back. 'As ordered, sir. Ready for sea.'

Bolitho knew he was being unfair to Egmont, but it sounded like a boast, as if he had manned and prepared the *Hotspur* for duty single-handed.

Verling snapped, 'Where is Mr. Sewell, our new midshipman? He should be here.'

Bolitho glanced at Dancer. Verling was back in his proper role. He even remembered the midshipman's name, when he could hardly have found time to meet him.

Egmont licked his lips. 'Below, sir. Being sick.' He licked his lips again. Just the mention of it in this choppy sea was having its effect.

Verling had not missed that, either.

'Dismiss the hands. We shall go aft. I trust the chart and

sailing instructions are ready, too?' He did not wait for an answer, but pulled out his watch and flicked open the guard with his thumbnail. 'So be it. The tide is right – we shall weigh at noon,' and to the thick-set boatswain's mate, 'Carry on, Tinker. You know your men.'

'Picked 'em meself, sir.'

Even the use of his nickname seemed correct and formal. Only Verling could have carried that off.

He stopped in his stride. 'Stow your gear, then report to me.' He saw Dancer peering around and added calmly, 'This is no line-of-battle ship, Mr. Dancer. I expect you to know every stay, block and spar by the time we drop anchor again!'

The deck lurched as the schooner snubbed at her anchor cable, and Dancer said quietly, 'Wind's getting up. Shan't be sorry when we do get under way.'

'A moment, you two!' It was Egmont, recovered, it seemed, from his performance earlier. 'I know both of you have just satisfied the Board – yesterday, wasn't it? And you heard what Mr. Verling said. Remember it well. Board or no Board, there'll be no passengers on this deck, *I'll* make certain of that. Now stow your gear and be sharp about it!'

They watched him turn away and gesticulate at some seamen, his words lost in the wind. Dancer shrugged.

'He needs a bigger ship, that one, if only for his head.'

Bolitho laughed.

'Let's go and find our fellow middy. I suspect it wasn't only the motion that made him vomit!'

Verling paused on the after ladder, his eyes level with the deck coaming.

It would be good to get away from the endless overhaul, clearing up disorder and making the ship, his ship, ready to take her place again, in response to any demand.

In *Gorgon* he was still the first lieutenant. Transferred to any other ship, he would be just another member of the wardroom, with seniority but no future.

He felt the hull shiver again, heard the clatter of loose rigging. She was alive. Eager to go.

He touched the shining paintwork. *So be it, then.*

As Tinker Thorne had firmly declared, the men chosen for *Hotspur*'s passage crew were all skilled and experienced hands, who would be badly missed if their old two-decker was suddenly ordered to sea.

Bolitho recognised most of them, and felt a sense of belonging which was hard to understand, although he had often heard older sailors describe it.

The initial unfamiliarity was gone at the moment of weighing anchor, with the first pressure of bodies leaning on the capstan bars, and the slow *clank, clank, clank* as the pawls started to respond. All spare hands thrusting in time to Tinker's hoarse commands. Midshipmen as well; even the cook in his white smock.

Two men on the wheel, others waiting to 'let go an' haul!' when the anchor broke free of the ground. Every piece of rigging joining the din, blocks taking the strain, ready for the canvas to fill and take command.

Verling stood by the compass box, his body poised for the moment of truth.

Clank, clank, clank, slower now.

A seaman, right forward above the bowsprit, peered aft and cupped his hands. Even so, his voice was almost drowned by the noise of wind and rigging.

He had seen the stout cable, now taut like a bar, and pointing directly at the stem. *Up-and-down.*

Then, 'Anchor's aweigh!'

It was something Bolitho would never forget. Nor want to. The sudden slackness on the capstan as the cable came home, the deck tilting, so steeply that the lee scuppers were awash as the hull continued to heel over.

It was exciting, awesome; not even in the lively revenue cutter *Avenger* had he known anything like it. The great sails cracking and filling to the wind, spray sluicing over them like icy rain. Feet sliding and kicking against the wet planking, gasps and curses from men bent almost double in the battle against wind and rudder.

Bolitho had watched plenty of smaller craft getting under way in a brisk wind. It had always fascinated and moved him, like seeing some great seabird spread its wings and lift from the water.

Even through and above the noise, he could hear Verling's occasional commands, could imagine him down aft by the wheel, angled against the tilt of the deck, watching each sail and the moving panorama of the land, blurred now as if seen through wet glass.

And over all Tinker Thorne's voice, urging, threatening.

'Catch another turn on that pin, Morgan! Move your bloody self, will you!'

Or, 'What d'you mean, Atkins, you *think*? Leave that to Jacks with brains!'

Bolitho saw the land, a white tower or beacon, bursting spray, rocks along the headland. A ship, too. Moving, anchored, or aground, it was impossible to tell. He knew Verling had put two leadsmen on either bow, a necessary precaution when leaving harbour for the first time, but it would take more than lead and line to save them if they misjudged the next cable or so.

'Over here!' Tinker again. 'You as well, Mr. Bolitho!' He was even managing to grin through the spray streaming down his leathery face. 'Remember what you was told, *no passengers*!'

Despite the movement and confusion Bolitho found he could smile, even laugh suddenly into the spray. The deck was steadier, the snaking halliards and braces stiff and taut in their blocks, and each great sail throwing its own pale reflection on the churning water alongside.

'Steady as you go!' Verling now, probably watching the final spur of headland. 'That will be Penlee Point.' He almost slipped, but a hand reached from somewhere and steadied him. The face he knew, but all he could gasp was, 'Bless you for that!'

The seaman ducked to avoid another snake of wet cordage as it hissed around its block and grinned. 'Do the same for me!' The grin widened. *'Sir!'*

The sky beyond the shrouds and hard canvas seemed

clearer, the motion still lively, but easier. Men were pausing at their work to look for a friend, relief, pride, something of each on their faces. Across the quarter the headland had fallen away and lost its menace. This time.

Bolitho gripped a backstay and took a deep breath.

Beyond the straining jib and staysails was open water: the Channel. He felt Dancer lurch against him, his hand on his shoulder.

Yesterday seemed a long way away. They were *free*.

5

Envy

Bolitho clambered through the main hatch, and seized a
stanchion as he steadied himself against the angle of the
deck and waited for his vision to clear. The night was pitch
black, the air and spray stinging his cheeks, driving away
all thoughts of sleep. And that was the odd thing, that he
was still wide awake. It was eight o'clock, and a full eight
hours since *Hotspur* had weighed anchor and struck south
into the Channel. The thrill and confusion, groping for
unfamiliar cordage and becoming more accustomed to the
schooner's demands in a brisk north-westerly wind, had
settled into a pattern of order and purpose.

They were divided into two watches, four hours on, four
off, with the dogwatches giving a brief respite in which to
devour a hot meal and fortify themselves with a tot of rum.
It all helped.

Verling was handing over the watch now, his tall shape just visible against the sliver of foam beyond the lee bulwark. 'Sou' east-by-south, Mr. Egmont. She should be steady a while now that the topsails are snug.' The merest pause, and Bolitho imagined him staring down at the junior lieutenant, making sure that there was no misunder-standing. 'Call me *immediately* if the sea gets up, or anything else happens that I ought to know.'

Bolitho moved closer to the wheel and the two helmsmen. He could see the bare feet of one, pale against the wet planking. During the first dogwatch he had seen the same seaman blowing onto his fingers to warm them against the bitter air, but he was standing barefoot now with no show of discomfort. He must have soles like leather.

Another shadow moved past the wheel and he saw a face catch the glow from the compass box: Andrew Sewell, the new midshipman. They had scarcely spoken since they had come aboard; Egmont had seen to that. Fifteen years old, Captain Conway had said. He looked younger. Nervous, shy, or possibly both, he was a pleasant-faced youth with fair skin and hazel eyes, and a quick smile that seemed only too rare. He had helped Bolitho lay out some charts in the precise way that Verling always seemed to expect. It had been then, in the poor light of the main cabin, that Bolitho had seen Sewell's hands. Scarred, torn and deeply bruised, never given the chance to become accustomed to the demands of seamanship. Deliberately driven seemed the most likely explanation; it was common enough even in today's navy. He remembered the captain's obvious concern for him, perhaps not merely because of his dead father.

Bolitho reached out impulsively and touched his elbow.

'Over here, Andrew! A bit more sheltered!' He felt him start to pull away, and added, 'Easy, now.'

Sewell let his arm go limp.

'I've just been sick again, Mister. . . .'

'"Dick" will do very well.' He waited, sensing the caution, the doubt. Sewell did not belong here. *Suppose I had felt like that when I was packed off to sea in* Manxman?

He looked up and watched the fine curve of the great sail above them. Not shapeless now, and pale blue in a shaft of light as the moon showed itself between banks of scudding cloud. And the sea, rising and falling like black glass, reaching out on either beam. Endless, with no horizon.

Bolitho tugged the rough tarpaulin coat away from his neck. It had rubbed his skin raw, but he had not noticed.

He said, 'This could be the middle of the Atlantic, or some other great ocean! And just us sailing across it, think of that.'

Sewell said, 'You mean that,' and hesitated, 'Dick? How you truly see it?'

'I suppose I do. I can't really explain. . . .' Something made him stop, like a warning, as he felt Sewell move slightly away.

'Nothing to do, then?' It was Egmont, almost invisible in a boat cloak against the black water and heavy cloud. 'I want a good watch kept *at all times*. Have you checked the deck log and the set course?'

Bolitho replied, 'Sou' east-by-south, sir. Helm is steady.'

Egmont turned toward Sewell.

'Did I hear you spewing up again? God help us all! I want you to check the glass yourself. Let every grain of sand run free before you turn it, see? I don't want you warming the glass every time, just so you can run below and dream of home. So do it!'

He glanced at the wheel as the spokes creaked again.

'Watch your helm, man! And stand up smartly, stay alert!' He swung away, the boat cloak floating around him. 'What's your name? I'll be watching *you*!'

The seaman shifted his bare feet on the grating.

'Archer.'

Egmont looked at Bolitho. 'I'm going below to check the chart. Watch the helm and call me if you need advice.'

He may have looked at the helmsman. 'And, Archer, say *sir* when you speak to an officer in the future!' He strode to the hatch.

Bolitho clenched his fist.

Then try to act like one!

He heard Sewell gasp, with surprise or disbelief, and realised that he had spoken aloud.

But he smiled, glad he was still able.

'Something else you've learned in *Hotspur, Mister* Sewell! Don't lose your temper so easily!'

Andrew Sewell, aged fifteen, and the only son of a hero, said nothing. It was like a hand reaching out, and he was no longer afraid to take it.

The helmsman named Archer called, 'Wind's gettin' up, sir!'

He jerked his head as the wet canvas rattled and cracked loudly above them.

Bolitho nodded. 'My respects to Mr. Egmont. . . .' The mood was still on him. '*No*. I'll tell him myself.'

Tired, elated, angry? Sailors often blamed it on the wind.

He reached the hatch and called back, 'Remember! *No passengers!*'

The wheel jerked sharply as both helmsmen gripped the spokes and put their weight against it, but the one named Archer managed to laugh.

'Easy does it, Tom. Our Dick's blood is on the boil. He'll see us right!'

Vague figures were moving to each mast, the watch on deck, and ready for the storm.

Andrew Sewell had heard the quick exchange between the two men at the wheel and felt something quite unknown to him. It was envy.

The next few hours were ones even the old Jacks were unlikely to forget. A blustery succession of squalls became a strong wind that had all hands fighting each onslaught, bruised and blinded by icy spray and the waves that burst across the bulwarks and swept down the scuppers like a tiderace. All through the middle watch the storm continued its assault, until even the most vociferous curses were beaten into silence.

But when the clouds eventually broke and a first hint of dawn showed itself against straining canvas and the criss-cross of shining rigging, *Hotspur* was holding her own, with not a spar or shroud broken.

Bolitho had remembered Tinker Thorne's admiration for her builder, Old John Barstow, *the finest in the West Country*; he had clung to those words more than once in the night when the sea had smashed against the hull or sent men sprawling like rag dolls in its wake.

Tinker's voice had rarely been silent, and his sturdy form was everywhere. Dragging a man from one task and shoving him into another, putting an extra pair of hands on halliard or brace, or bullying another too dazed to think clearly, to add his weight to the pumps.

And Verling was always there. Down aft, holding himself upright, while he watched the relentless battle of sea against rudder, wind against canvas.

A few men were injured, but none seriously, with cuts and bruises, or rope burns when human hands could no longer control wet cordage squealing through block or cleat.

And as suddenly as it had begun, the wind eased, and it was safe to move about the deck without pain or apprehension.

Bolitho heard Verling say, 'Another hour, Mr. Egmont, and we'll get the tops'ls on her. The wind's backed a piece. I want a landfall on Guernsey, not the coast of France!' Calmly said, but he was not joking. 'Check and report any damage. Injuries, too. I'll need it for my report.' He patted the compass box. 'Not bad for a youngster, eh?'

Egmont hurried forward, his boat cloak plastered to his body like a mould. In the poor light it was hard to gauge his reaction to the storm.

''Ere, sir.' Bolitho felt a mug pushed into his frozen fingers. 'Get yer blood movin' again!'

Rum, cognac, it could have been anything, but it began to work instantly.

'Thank you, Drury – just in time!' The seaman laughed. Like Bolitho, he was probably surprised that he had remembered his name.

Dancer joined him by the foremast and clapped his shoulder.

'Well, that's all over, Dick!' His smile was very white against wind-seared features. ''Til the next time!'

They both looked up. The masthead pendant was just visible against the banks of low cloud, flicking out like a coachman's whip, but not bar-taut as it must have been for the past few hours.

Dancer said, 'I'll not be sorry to see the sun again!'

'*Here?* In January?' They both laughed, and a sailor who was squatting by the forward hatch while his leg was being bandaged stared up at them and grinned.

Tinker had heard Verling's words to Egmont, and Bolitho saw that he was already mustering some of his topmen, getting ready to loose the topsails. *Hotspur* would fly when that was done. Like the great seabird of his imagination.

'Go below, one of you, and fetch my glass!'

Bolitho called, 'Aye, sir!' and nudged his friend's arm. 'You stay and watch for the sun!' Dancer's coat sleeve was heavy with spray.

Dancer saw the question in his eyes and shrugged. 'I put my tarpaulin over one of the injured.'

Bolitho said, 'You would!'

It was deserted below deck, although he could hear men shouting to one another as they put new lashings on some of the stores *Hotspur* was carrying as additional ballast. He paused to listen to the sea, sluicing and thudding against the hull. Quieter now, but still menacing, showing its power.

He found Verling's telescope, just inside the tiny cabin which would be the new master's domain and, when necessary, his retreat.

Verling's coat was hanging on a hook, swaying with the motion like a restless spectre. When *Hotspur* anchored again, he would go ashore as a well turned-out sea officer, not as a survivor. It was impossible to see him in any other light.

He stiffened, surprised that he had not heard it before. Sewell's voice, husky, even cowed.

'I *didn't*, sir. I was only trying to. . . .'

He got no further, cut short by Egmont, angry, malicious, sarcastic.

'What d' you mean, *you couldn't help it*? You make me sick, and you still believe that anybody will ever accept *you* for a commission?' He was laughing now; Bolitho could see him in his mind. Barely out of the midshipmen's berth himself, and he was behaving like a tyrant.

'I've been watching you, and do you think I've not guessed what you're trying to do?' There was another sound. A slap. 'And if I see you again. . . .'

Bolitho did not know he had moved. It was like the actors in the square at Falmouth; they had all watched them as children, had cheered or hissed to match the mimes and poses.

Egmont swinging round to stare at him, mouth half open, cut short by the interruption, one hand still in the air, after the blow, or preparing another. Sewell, leaning against the curved timbers, covering his cheek or mouth, but his eye fixed on Bolitho.

'What th' hell are you doing here?'

Almost as if he had imagined it. Egmont quite calm now, arms at his sides, swaying to the motion, but in control. And the young midshipman, saying nothing, his face guarded, expressionless. Only the red welt by his mouth as evidence.

Bolitho said, 'I came for the first lieutenant's glass.' It was like hearing someone else. Clipped, cold. Like Hugh.

'Well, don't just stand there! Take it and go!'

Bolitho looked past him. 'Are you all right, Andrew?'

Sewell swallowed, and seemed unable to speak. Then he nodded and exclaimed, 'Yes, of course. It was nothing, you see. . . .'

Egmont snapped, 'Hold your tongue!' and turned to Bolitho again. 'Go about your duties. I'll overlook your insolence this time, but. . . .' He did not finish it, but swung round and left the cabin.

They stood facing each other, without speaking or moving, the sounds of rigging and sea distant, unintrusive.

'Tell me, Andrew.' Bolitho reached out to take his arm, and saw him flinch as if he expected another blow. 'He *struck* you, and just before that. . . .'

He got no further.

'No. It would only make things worse. D'you think I don't know? What it's like – *really* like?'

Bolitho felt the anger rising like fire. Egmont's shock when he had burst into this cabin, and then as quickly, his recovery and arrogance. He could still feel Sewell's arm; it was shaking. Fear? It went deeper than that.

He said, 'I'll come aft with you right now. Mr. Verling will listen. He *has* to. And in any case. . . .'

But Sewell was shaking his head.

'*No.*' He looked at him directly for the first time. 'It wouldn't help.' Then, quite firmly, he pried Bolitho's fingers from his arm. 'He would deny it. And . . . so would I.'

Someone was shouting; feet thudded across the deck overhead. He still held Verling's telescope in his other hand. Nothing was making sense.

Sewell was fumbling with his coat, trying to fasten his buttons, not looking at him now. 'You will be a good officer, Dick, a fine one. I see the way they respect you, and *like* you. I always hoped. . . .'

He moved abruptly to the door, and to the ladder beyond.

Bolitho stood very still, his anger giving way to a sense of utter defeat. Because of what he had just seen and heard, and because it mattered.

There were more shouts, and he found himself on the ladder as if it were an escape. But he kept seeing Sewell's face, and his fear. He needed help. *And I failed him.*

On deck, it seemed nothing had happened, routine taking over as seamen jostled at their stations for making more sail. *Hotspur* had altered course again, the canvas shivering and cracking, the main and gaff topsails taut across the bulwark, throwing broken reflections across the water alongside.

'Loose tops'ls! Lively there!'

Verling called, 'Give it to me!' He seized the telescope and trained it across the weather bow. 'Thought you'd fallen outboard. Where the hell were you?' He did not wait for an answer or seem to expect one, and was already calling to men by the foremast.

Egmont was near the wheel, shading his eyes to peer up at the topsail yards. He glanced only briefly at Bolitho before returning his attention to the newly released sails as they filled and hardened to the wind. Disinterested. Bolitho heard Sewell's voice again. *He would deny it. And so would I.*

'All secure, sir!' That was Tinker, eyes like slits as he stared at the small figures on the yards, groping their way back to safety.

Most of the sea was still hidden in darkness, but the sky was lighter, and in so short a time the vessel had taken shape and regained her personality around and above them, faces and voices emerging from groups and shadows.

Bolitho felt the deck plunge beneath him, exuberant, like the wild creature she was. *Hotspur* would make a fine and graceful sight even in this poor light, with all sails set and filled, the yards bending like bows under the strain.

'Now that was *something*, Dick!' It was Dancer, hatless, his fair hair plastered across a forehead gleaming with spray.

Verling said, 'Send half of the hands below, Mr. Egmont. Get some food into them. And don't be too long about it.' His mind was already moving on. 'Two good masthead lookouts.' He must have sensed a question, and added, 'One man sees only what he expects to see if he's left alone too long.' His arm shot out. 'Mr. Bolitho, *you* stand by. I need some keen eyes this morning!' He might even have smiled. 'This is no two-decker!'

Bolitho felt his stomach muscles tighten. Even the mention of climbing aloft could still make his skin crawl.

Verling was saying, 'Take my glass with you. I'll tell you what to watch out for.'

Dancer said softly, 'I hope I'm as confident as he is when I'm told to take a ship from one cross on the chart to another. Nothing ever troubles *him*.'

They went below, and suddenly he grasped Bolitho's arm and pulled him against the galley bulkhead.

'I've been thinking. You remember what Captain Conway said about young Sewell's experiences in previous

66

ships? One of them was the *Ramillies*, wasn't it, in the Downs Squadron? Where everything started to go against him.'

Bolitho said nothing, waiting. It was as if Dancer had just been with him. Then he said cautiously, 'What about *Ramillies*?'

'Something I heard a minute ago made me stop and think. Surprised Conway didn't know.' He turned as if to listen as someone hurried past. 'Our Mister Egmont was a middy on board at the same time as Sewell. A bully even then, to all accounts.'

More figures were slipping and clattering down the ladder, jostling one another and laughing, fatigue and injuries forgotten until the next call.

Bolitho said, 'Then I've just made an enemy,' and told him what had happened.

Someone ducked his head through the hatch. Bolitho could see his face clearly despite the lingering gloom between decks.

'What is it?'

'Mr. Verling wants you on deck, sir.' A quick grin. ' "Fast as you like", 'e says!'

In the silence that followed, Dancer said lightly, 'Then I'm sorry to say Egmont's made another enemy. He seems to have a talent for it.'

They reached the upper deck together. There was more cloud than earlier, rain too.

Dancer exclaimed, 'Thunder! Not another storm, I hope.'

Bolitho looked at him. The bond between them was even stronger.

'Not on your oath, Martyn. That was cannon fire!'

6

No Quarter

The deck seemed unusually crowded, all thought of rest and food forgotten. Some men were in the bows, peering or gesturing ahead, calling to one another, voices distorted by the wind. Others had climbed into the shrouds, but the sea was still dark and empty. And there was no more gunfire.

Verling said, 'Due south of us.' His eye lit up as he gazed into the compass. 'Dead ahead, if I'm not mistaken.'

'At least we can outsail 'em, sir.' That was Tinker.

Egmont snapped, 'We're not at *war*, man!'

Verling glanced at him. 'We take no chances, Mr. Egmont. Today's handshake can easily become tomorrow's broadside.'

Dancer murmured, 'What do you think, Dick? Heavy guns?'

Bolitho shook his head. 'Big enough. There was no

return fire.' Ships meeting by accident, a case of mistaken identity in the darkness and foul weather. These were busy trade routes where almost any flag might be sighted. And the possibility of war was never forgotten. *Shoot first*, was often the first rule.

Smugglers, privateers, or local pirates, every deepwater sailor had to take his chance.

Bolitho looked over toward Verling and tried to see it as he would. Facing an unknown threat, considering his own responsibility. The officer in charge . . . He had heard it said all too frequently. Do wrong and you carried the blame. Do right, and if you were too junior, others reaped the praise.

Deliver Hotspur *to her new command, and return to Plymouth without unnecessary delay.* The orders were plain enough. Maybe Verling was weighing the choices that might lie ahead. Fight or run, as Tinker had suggested. *Hotspur* carried two small bow-chasers, six-pounders, quite enough to deal with trouble in home waters. But no shot had yet been brought aboard. And her four swivel guns would be useless in any serious engagement.

Verling had made up his mind.

'Stand by to shorten sail. Reef tops'ls and take in the gaff tops'l.' Another glance at the compass. Bolitho could see his face now without the aid of the lamp. The sky was clearing, the clouds purple toward the horizon, when it was visible.

He heard Egmont ask, 'Shall we fight, sir?'

Verling was gesturing to Dancer. 'Fetch my logbook,

then stand by me.' He seemed to recall the question. 'We've no marines to support us this time. Break open the arms chest.' He did not even raise his voice.

He looked at Bolitho. 'Up you go. Sweep to the sou' east. Take your time. Remember what you saw on the chart.'

Afterwards, Bolitho recalled how each point was allowed to settle in his mind, take shape. So calmly said when Verling's entire being must have wanted to ram his meaning home, or even to snatch up the glass and claw his way aloft himself. In case he was mistaken. When Bolitho and the other midshipmen had gathered around *Gorgon*'s sailing master, old Turnbull, for their regular instruction in navigation and pilotage, or when they were struggling with the mysteries of the sextant, they had often been warned about the first sight of land. Turnbull had reminded his youthful audience, 'An error in judgment is no excuse at the court-martial table!'

He reached the foremast shrouds as Verling shouted, 'Shorten sail!'

Men were already at their stations, handling lines and tackles as if they had been serving *Hotspur* for months, not days.

Bolitho climbed steadily but slowly, making sure each ratline was underfoot before he took his weight with his arms, Verling's heavy telescope thumping across his spine. He heard Tinker call after him, 'Don't drop *that*, me son, or the sky'll fall on you!'

How he could find time to joke about it was a marvel. Tinker was everywhere, and at once. Ready to help or threaten without hesitation. He should have been promoted to warrant rank; there was not a strand of rope or strip of sail he could not control. But in twenty-five years at sea, he had never learned to read or write.

Bolitho reached the upper yard, and could feel his heart banging against his ribs. *Too long in harbour. Getting soft.* . . .

The lookout already curled in position, his arm around a stay, turned and peered at him.

'Mornin', sir!' He jerked his thumb. 'Land, larboard bow!'

Bolitho swallowed and forced himself to look. Sea and haze, an endless expanse of choppy white crests. But no land.

The lookout was one of *Gorgon*'s foretopmen; more to the point, he had been chosen by Tinker for the passage crew.

He gasped, 'Tell them, Keveth! No breath!'

He swung the telescope carefully around and beneath his arm, even as the lookout yelled to the small figures below. With a name like that, he must be a fellow Cornishman. Two wreckers up here together. . . .

He opened the telescope with great care, waiting for each roll and shudder running through his perch, causing *Hotspur* to vibrate from truck to keel.

Land, sure enough. Another careful breath, gauging the moment. The sea breaking; he could feel the power and height of the waves, but when he lowered the glass to clear his vision there was nothing there. *But it was there.* The blunt outline of land, sloping to a point which defied the waves. Like the little sketch in Verling's log.

Jerbourg Point. Who or what was 'Jerbourg', he wondered.

He made his way down to the deck and hurried aft, slipped and almost fell, lightheaded, as if drunk or in fever.

Verling listened as he blurted out everything he had seen. He was conscious of his eyes, his patience, as he described the landfall.

All he said was, 'Well done.'

Egmont said loudly, 'I'll note it in the log, sir.'

Bolitho said, 'The lookout, Keveth. *He* sighted it first, sir. Without a glass!'

Verling glanced at both of them, as usual missing nothing.

'A good hand, that one. A fair shot, too, when given the chance.' The hint of a smile. 'And should be. He was a poacher before he signed up with a recruiting party. One jump ahead of the hangman, I shouldn't wonder.'

'Deck there!' It was the masthead again. The poacher. *'Wreckage ahead, larboard bow!'*

Verling did not hesitate. As if he had been expecting it; as if he knew.

'Stand by to lower a boat. Two leadsmen in the chains.' His hand shot out. 'Good ones, Tinker. This is no coastline for chances.'

Egmont asked, 'You know Guernsey, sir?'

'I've sailed close by before.' He was looking toward the land, which was still invisible. 'It was enough.'

He walked to the hatch. 'Wreckage. Wind and tide make their own landfalls, for *us*, eh?'

Dancer commented softly, 'My God, he keeps a cool head!' He clasped Bolitho's arm. 'Like another ancient mariner not a cable's length away!'

It seemed to take an age for the drifting fragments of wreckage to become clearly visible, more scattered, and reaching out on either bow. There was absolute silence now, the seamen very aware of their kinship with these pathetic remnants which had once been a living vessel.

Verling was on deck again, and stood with his arms folded, watching the sea, and the strengthening blur of land which had almost been forgotten.

Hotspur had shortened sail once more, so that her shipboard sounds in the silence added to the atmosphere of uneasiness, with the creak and clatter of loose rigging, and the groan of the rudder and yoke-lines as the helmsmen fought to maintain steerage way.

Verling said, 'I think both boats will be necessary. It will save time. Not that there is much to see.' He was thinking aloud, as if questioning each thought as it came to him.

Even Tinker's voice seemed subdued as he watched the first boat being hoisted and swung above and over the gunwale.

Verling said, 'You leave now, Mr. Egmont. See what you can discover. Small craft, I'd say.'

Egmont leaned over the side as some larger fragments of timber bumped against *Hotspur*'s side.

Bolitho felt a chill run through him. It was, or had been,

a cutter as far as he could tell. Like *Avenger* . . . There was part of a mast now, and torn sail dragging half-submerged, like a shroud.

The first boat was pulling away, with Egmont in the bows, leaning over to signal his intentions to his coxswain.

Verling called, 'Now you, Bolitho.' He had his glass up to his eye again, but trained on the spur of land, not the splintered remains drifting below him. 'Take Sewell with you. Stay up to wind'rd if you can.'

He felt as if he were being cut off, abandoned, once the boat was in the water and the headrope cast off.

'Easy, lads, keep it steady!' He had taken the tiller himself and waited for the oars to pick up the stroke, each man feeling the mood of the sea, trying not to watch the schooner as she fell further and further astern.

At least the wind had eased. Bolitho felt the salt spray on his mouth and soaking into his shoulders. Sewell was crouched down beside him, his back half turned; impossible to see or know what he was thinking. Hard to believe that the confrontation in the cabin had ever happened. Only this was real.

He winced as the boat dipped steeply and more spray burst from the oars. This was no cutter or gig built for the open sea.

'*There!*' Sewell's arm shot out. 'Oh, God, it's one of them!'

Bolitho stood up, holding fast to the tiller-bar to keep his balance.

'Bowman! Use your hook!'

The seaman had boated his oar and was poised in the blunt bows like a harpoonist as more wreckage surged above a trough.

'Oars! Fend off, lads!'

It was as if a complete section of the wreck had risen suddenly and violently from the depths, like some act of retribution or spite.

An oar blade splintered and the seaman pitched across his thwart, the broken loom still grasped in his fists. Surprisingly, nobody shouted or showed any sign of fear. It was too swift, too stark. Not just one corpse, but five or six, tangled together in a mesh of torn canvas and broken planking.

It lasted only a few seconds, before the corpses and their tangled prison rolled over and dipped beneath the sea.

Only seconds, but as they fought to bring the boat under command again, the grim picture remained. Staring eyes, bared teeth, gaping wounds, black in the hard light. And the stench of gunpowder. Like the splinters and the burns: they had been fired upon at point-blank range.

Bolitho tugged at the tiller-bar. 'Back water, starboard!' He felt the sea sluicing around his legs, as if the boat had been swamped and was going down.

He heard Sewell yell, 'More wreckage!' He was clambering over the struggling oarsmen, thrusting his legs over the side to fend off another piece of broken timber. Then he must have lost his footing, and slithered bodily over the gunwale, his face contorted with pain.

The seaman who had been in the bows flung himself

over the thwart and seized his arm, just as Bolitho managed to bring the boat under control.

Nobody spoke; nothing mattered but the slow, steady splash of oars as they regained the stroke and gave all their strength to the fight. Only then did they turn and peer at each other, more gasps than grins, but with the recognition that, this time, they had won.

Bolitho eased the tiller very slowly, feeling the effort of each stroke, knowing they were in control.

Sewell lay in the sternsheets, the trapped water surging across his legs, his lip bleeding where he had bitten through it. Bolitho reached down and wrenched opcn his coat. His breeches were torn; it must have happened when he had used both legs to kick off that last piece of wreckage. But for his prompt action, the boat might have foundered.

There was blood, too, a lot of it. He could feel the torn skin, the muscle under his fingers clenched against the pain.

He exclaimed, 'You mad little bugger!'

Pain, shock, and the bitter cold; Sewell was barely able to form the words.

'I was drowning . . . I couldn't h-hold on. My fault. . . .'

He cried out as Bolitho knotted a piece of wet rag around his leg, the blood strangely vivid in the grey light.

Bolitho pulled some canvas across his body and shouted, 'You saved the boat! Did you think we'd just *leave* you?' He was gripping his shoulder now, as if to force him to understand.

'I just wanted to. . . .' He fainted.

Bolitho swung the tiller-bar against his ribs until the impact steadied him.

'Enough, lads! Give way, *together*!'

The boat lifted and swayed as the blades brought her under command again. Bolitho clung to Sewell's sodden coat to ease the shock of each sudden plunge.

He heard himself gasp, 'I *know* what you wanted! I'll remind you when we get back on board!'

Someone yelled, ''Ere's *'Otspur*, sir! Larboard beam!'

Bolitho wiped his streaming face with his wrist, his eyes raw with salt. A blurred shape, like a sketch on a slate. Unreal. He tugged at Sewell's coat and gasped, 'See? We found her!'

The rest was a confused daze, the schooner's shining side rising over them like a breakwater, muffled shouts, and figures leaping down to take the strain and fasten the tackles for hoisting the boat into what suddenly seemed a stable and secure haven. He felt a fist thumping his shoulder, heard Tinker's familiar, harsh voice.

'Well done, me boy!' Another thump. 'Bloody well done!'

Then, almost choking over a swallow of raw spirit. Rum, cognac; it could have been anything. But it was working. He could feel every scrape and bruise, but his mind was clearing, like a mist lifting from the sea.

And Verling. Calm, level, a little less patient now.

'What did you find?'

It was all suddenly very sharp. Brutal . . . Like the end of a nightmare. Even the sounds of sea and wind seemed muffled. The ship holding her breath.

'They were all dead, sir. Killed. Point-blank range.' Like listening to somebody else, the voice flat and contained. 'No chance. Taken by surprise, you see.' He could see their faces, the savage wounds and staring eyes. Not a drawn blade or weapon in sight. *Cut down.* 'Grape and canister.' He broke off, coughing, and a hand held a cloth to his mouth. Only a piece of rag, but it seemed strangely warm. Safe.

He knew it was Dancer.

Verling again. 'Anything more?'

Bolitho licked his raw lips. He said, 'There were two officers. I saw their clothes.' The image was fading. 'Their buttons. Officers.'

Verling said, 'Take him below.' His hand touched Bolitho's arm briefly. 'You behaved well. Anything else that comes back to you. . . .'

He was already turning away, his mind grappling with other questions. Bolitho struggled to sit up.

'Sewell saved the boat, sir. He might have been killed.'

Verling had stopped and was staring down at him, his face in shadow against the fast-moving clouds. '*You* did nothing, of course.' Somebody even laughed.

Bolitho was on his feet now. He could feel the deck. Alive again. He should be shivering. Holding on. He was neither.

Dancer was saying, 'When I saw the boat, I thought. . . .' He did not continue. Could not.

Bolitho held on to a backstay and looked at the sea. A

deep swell, unbroken now but for a few white horses. No wreckage; not even a splinter to betray what had happened.

And the dark wedge of land, no nearer, or so it seemed. And yet it reached out on either bow, lifting and falling against *Hotspur*'s standing and running rigging, as if it, and not the schooner, was moving.

Dancer said, 'Young Sewell seems to be holding out well. I heard the lads say you saved his skin, or most of it. He'll never forget this day, I'll wager!' He added bitterly, 'Of course, Egmont's boat found nothing!'

They were standing in the cabin space, although Bolitho could not recall descending the ladder. Here the ship noises were louder, closer. Creaks and rattles, the sigh of the sea against the hull.

Bolitho turned and stared at his friend, seeing him as if for the first time since he had been hauled aboard.

'We might never have known, but for the gunfire. It was the merest chance.' He held up his arm and saw that the sleeve was torn from wrist to elbow. He had felt nothing. 'We can't simply sail past and forget it, as if nothing has happened!'

Dancer shook his head. 'It's up to the first lieutenant, Dick. I was watching him just now. He'll not turn his back on it.' He regarded him grimly. 'He can't. Even if he wanted to.'

Someone called his name, and he said, 'We'll soon know. I'm just thankful you're still in one piece.' He was trying to smile, but it eluded him. Instead, he lightly punched the torn sleeve. 'Young Andy Sewell has you to look up to now!'

He swung away to find out who had called him. 'That makes two of us!'

Bolitho stood by the cabin door, and tried to calm his thoughts, put them in order. Fear, anger, relief. And something else. It was pride.

'Ah, here you are, *sir!*' It was Tinker, almost filling the space. He had a cutlass under one arm, and was holding out a slim-bladed hanger with his other hand. 'More to your fancy, I thought.' He was grinning, although watching him keenly. 'Mister Verling's orders. Seems we're goin' after the bastards!'

Who? Where? With what? It had never been in doubt.

Feet thumped overhead and Bolitho heard the impatient squeal of blocks, the flap and bang of canvas free in the wind. *Hotspur* was under way once more.

Verling's decision, right or wrong. For him, there was no choice.

Tinker nodded slowly, as if reading his thoughts. 'Are ye ready?'

Bolitho could hear Verling's voice, Egmont's too. But he was thinking of the staring, dead faces in the water.

He fastened the belt at the waist and allowed the hanger to fall against his thigh.

Tomorrow's enemy. He said, 'Aye. So be it.'

7

Command Decision

Lieutenant Montagu Verling stood by the cabin table, his head slightly bent between the deck beams, his face in shadow. The fingers of his left hand rested only lightly on the table while his body swayed to the schooner's motion. Even that seemed easier; you could almost feel the nearness of land. Something physical. Outside, the sky, like the sea, was grey, and the wind, although steady, had dropped. The sails were heavy with rain and spray.

Here in the cabin, the light was no better, despite a couple of lamps. Verling's chart was spread almost directly beneath the small cabin skylight, strangely clear as it appeared to move slowly from side to side with each steady roll.

Bolitho saw the brass dividers in Verling's right hand move again, the points tapping the chart. Perhaps he was reconsidering, ensuring he had forgotten nothing, sifting fact and speculation.

Bolitho glanced at Dancer. The quill in his hand had hesitated, poised over his log and the record of events he was keeping for Verling. Achievement, or a legal defense; all would depend on the next few hours.

Verling had turned slightly, and the angle freed his features of shadow. He looked calm and alert, as if he were quite alone here, and this was just another day.

Bolitho wanted to turn and look once more around the cabin, record the images in his mind, and the others who were sharing this moment. Dancer, opposite, with the open log, the ink on the page already dry, the writing, the sloping, cultured hand he had come to know so well. He could imagine it that of a captain, perhaps even a flag officer, making some comment for posterity on the occasion of some great battle at sea. Beside Dancer, staring at the chart although his eyes were scarcely moving, Lieutenant Egmont, the corners of his mouth turned down. What was he thinking, feeling? Impatience, doubt, or fear?

And Midshipman Andrew Sewell, lying propped on a bench seat, his bandaged legs thrust out, his eyes tightly shut. When he awoke from the oblivion of pain and rum, he would be different, *feel* different. Another chance awaited him. He might even come to accept the life he had not chosen, lived though it must be in his father's far-reaching shadow.

The door creaked, and without looking Bolitho knew it was Tinker Thorne blocking the passageway, sharing the meeting but, as always, with an ear tuned to the ship, the sounds of sea, wind and rigging clearer to him than any chart or conference of war.

Bolitho touched the hanger that lay against his leg. And they were *not* at war. That must be uppermost in Verling's mind at this very moment. He looked up, and realised that Verling was staring directly at him, but when he spoke it was to all of them. And to the ship, which should have been delivered to St. Peter Port on Guernsey's east coast today, as stated in his orders.

'It is obvious that whatever vessel was responsible for so ruthless and unprovoked an attack on the cutter was already engaged in some unlawful mission. Smuggling is too commonplace between these islands and the mainland to provoke such an attack, or the murder of unprepared sailors and their officers.'

Egmont said, 'I didn't see them, sir. But if Mr. Bolitho says otherwise. . . .'

Verling interjected, 'You will *what*?'

In the silence that followed, he tapped the chart with his dividers.

'You don't have to be told that these are dangerous waters. Among these reefs and shallows, pilotage is often a dire necessity, even for visitors familiar with this coast-line.' His eyes returned to Bolitho. 'Those men who were killed had not been preparing to fight or to withstand an attack, correct?'

Dancer's pen was moving again, the scratching quite audible above the sounds of the hull and the sea.

'Correct, sir.'

Verling nodded. 'Which is *why* they were killed. Because they recognised the other vessel.'

'Local smugglers, sir?' He shook his head. 'Then why the force of arms, the point-blank range?'

Egmont cleared his throat and said stiffly, 'Mistaken identity perhaps, sir?' When Verling did not answer, he hurried on, 'We can proceed to St. Peter Port and hand over *Hotspur* as planned. Warn the garrison – they can send troopers overland, or maybe there will be some local patrol vessel armed and ready to deal with this intruder.' His eyes flicked over Bolitho. 'Smuggler, or the like.'

Dancer laid down his pen and said quietly, 'I learned a good deal about local trade, sir. My father used to instruct me on the subject. Gin from Rotterdam, brandy from France and Spain, rum from the West Indies. Some five to six million gallons of it were imported each year.' He looked up at Verling, the blue eyes very clear. 'And tobacco from Virginia. All for sale to our own traders,' he paused, 'and smugglers. It made St. Peter Port rich. Adventurous.'

Egmont said scornfully, 'I don't see that your boyhood lessons in "local trade" can be of any interest here!'

Dancer did not look at him; he was speaking only to Verling. 'My father also dealt with a number of ships which traded in tea.'

Egmont looked as if he were about to burst out laughing, but stifled it abruptly as Verling said, 'You have a good brain, Mr. Dancer. I can see why your father had a rather different course charted for you.' He banged the table with his knuckles. 'Ships familiar with these waters, but suitable for the ocean as well. And big enough to carry powerful guns for self-defense,' he looked around the cabin, 'or murder.'

He swung away from the table. 'Call all hands. We will change tack directly. Then have the people lay aft. They shall hear what we are about, and what I intend!'

He strode to the adjoining cabin and closed the door.

Dangerous, reckless; many would say irresponsible.

Bolitho looked over at Dancer, now closing the log.

Certainly the bravest.

Bolitho tightened his neckcloth and winced at the water running on his skin, soaking his shoulder. Rain or spray, it made no difference now. He stared along the glistening deck, beyond the foremast and flapping canvas to the land, the rugged outline of which seemed to stretch from bow to bow. It, too, was blurred by a heavier belt of rain sweeping out to meet them.

Verling was taking no unnecessary chances, with topsails reefed and a minimum of canvas, and a leadsman in the chains on either bow.

Even now he heard one of them call out, *'No bottom, sir!'*

Plenty of room for any shift of tack. So far. But he knew from the chart how swiftly that could change. There were sandbars, and a scattered necklace of reef less than a mile distant.

He glanced over his sodden shoulder at the helmsmen, eyes slitted against the downpour as they peered up at the shaking canvas and the vague shadow of the masthead pendant, barely lifting in the wind. Verling was close by, hands behind his back, hat pulled low over his forehead.

What was he thinking now? The seamen at their stations, wet and shivering, were probably hating him, although an hour ago, even less, he had seen some of them nod with approval; a couple had even raised a cheer. The grim remains of the cutter and its crew had been stark in each man's mind.

This was different. Sailors took risks every day, although few would admit it. They obeyed orders; it was their life. But suppose Verling was wrong, and he was taking an unnecessary risk with *Hotspur*, and the life of every man aboard?

He watched Verling walk unhurriedly to the weather bulwark and back to the compass box.

One day that might be me. Could I do it?

He felt, rather than saw, Dancer move across the slippery planking to join him.

'D' you think we're too late?'

Dancer was closer now, his voice just loud enough to be heard over the downpour and the shudder of rigging.

'Not unless they turned and ran immediately after the attack. But they must know these waters well.' He stared toward the land as a tall column of surf rose against a darker backdrop, before falling slowly.

Soundless, like a giant spectre. 'They'd not last a dog watch otherwise!'

Bolitho shivered, but found a strange comfort in his friend's words.

Dancer looked round as Egmont's voice cut through the other noises. Men were already running to obey his orders.

'*He'll* probably be proved right in the end.'

He bit his lip as the call came aft again from the chains.

'*By th' mark ten, sir!*'

Bolitho imagined the leadsman feverishly coiling in the wet line and preparing for another heave. He tried to picture *Hotspur*'s keel dipping and lifting through the depths of grey sea. Ten fathoms. Sixty feet. Safe enough. So far. . . .

'No bottom, sir!'

He let out a sigh of relief. No wonder experienced sailors treated the Channel Islands with such respect and caution.

Verling strode past them, one hand covering the lens of his telescope. Perhaps he had changed his mind. Remembered tomorrow in St. Peter Port, this might seem an act of reckless folly.

'Mr. Egmont, we will come about directly! Muster your anchor party.'

He had not changed his mind.

'*By th' mark seven!*'

Verling had trained his glass on the spur of headland, legs braced as he gauged the distance and bearing. Bolitho saw his face as he turned to watch the seamen crouching on the forecastle above the cathead. *Hotspur* was already coming about and into the wind, sails in confusion and, suddenly, all aback.

'Let go!'

Bolitho tried to see the chart in his mind; he and Dancer had pored over it and gone through Verling's notes until they almost knew them by heart.

The cable was still running out, the anchor plunging down, and down. A sandy bottom here, sheltered in its way by the same reef which had thrown up an occasional giant wave.

More men were scampering to secure sheets and braces, the deck swaying heavily as the anchor's fluke gripped and the cable took the full strain.

Dancer had his hand to his mouth. He had cut it at some time, but he was already running to add his strength to the others'.

Tinker cupped his hands. *'All secure, sir!'*

Hotspur had come to her anchor, her masts tall against sullen cloud. Even the wind had dropped, or so it seemed. Bolitho looked at the land. Once only a pencilled cross on Verling's chart; now a blurred reality through the lens of a telescope.

He wiped the stinging spray from his eyes. So hard to believe. It was no time at all since he had first seen *Hotspur*, and had heard Dancer say, 'I'll not want to leave this beauty when the time comes!'

And that would not be long now, no matter what diversion delayed them. The way ahead was clear.

He heard Egmont shouting names, saw Tinker standing

at his elbow, nodding or making some encouraging comment as a man responded and snatched up cutlass or musket.

He had seen all this before, and should be hardened to it. Eyes seeking out a friendly face: those you fought for when battle was joined. But he was still not used to it, and was moved by it. Perhaps he was not alone, and others felt it also, and concealed it.

Someone muttered, 'I'll lay a bet them bastards is watchin' us right now, as we breathe!'

Another laughed. 'Not if I sees the scumbags first!'

Was that all it took?

And suddenly there was no more time left. One boat was hard alongside, swaying and lurching in the swell, men clambering down sure-footed, as if it were part of a drill.

Verling stood with his back to the sea, as if unwilling to let them go.

He said, 'Find out what you can.' He was looking at Egmont, as if they had the deck to themselves. 'I must know the strength and position of the enemy. But remember, no heroics. If you cannot find or identify the other vessel, stand fast until I send help, or recall you.' His glance moved only briefly to Bolitho. 'It is important. So take care.'

Egmont half turned, and swung back.

'It might take hours to make our way across to the anchorage, sir.'

'I know. There is no alternative.' He reached out as if to touch the lieutenant's arm, but decided against it. 'I shall be

90

here. Conceal the boat as soon as you get ashore.' He saw a seaman signalling from the bulwark, and said curtly, 'Off with you.'

Bolitho scrambled into position but hesitated as Dancer leaned toward him, his face only inches away.

'Easy does it, Dick. Glory can wait,' he was trying to grin, 'until *I'm* with you!'

And then Bolitho was in the boat, wedged against the tiller-bar with Egmont beside him. The boat was full, two men to an oar, the bottom boards strewn with weapons and some hastily packed rations.

He heard Tinker shout, 'Cast off! *Easy*, lads!' He would be remaining aboard, hating it. But Verling was short-handed, and if another squall found them or *Hotspur* was forced to up-anchor for some reason, Tinker would be the key to survival.

The oars rose and dipped, slowly but steadily. It was going to be a hard pull.

Egmont shouted, 'Watch the stroke, damn you! Together now!'

Bolitho looked over his shoulder. *Hotspur* was already beyond reach.

Egmont said, 'Take over, will you? Steer for the ridge.' He swore under his breath as spray dashed over the stem and drifted aft. It was like ice. 'Of all the damn stupid ideas. . . .'

He did not finish it.

Bolitho tried to guess what lay ahead, and to hold the image of the coastline fixed in his mind.

He called, 'Be ready with the boat's lead-and-line –' and paused, fixing a name to the face. 'Price, isn't it?'

'Indeed it is, sir! And I'm ready!' He sounded as if it were a joke, and the Welsh accent was very pronounced.

He heard Egmont mutter something. Anger or anxiety, he could not tell. He was a stranger, and would always remain so.

And Verling; was he having second thoughts now that he had set his plan in motion? Suppose there was no other vessel, no 'enemy'? He would be reprimanded for hazarding *Hotspur* to no purpose. And if he had sent a landing party into real danger, the blame would be immediate. He recalled Verling's face when he had turned to watch *Gorgon* as they had weighed anchor at Plymouth. As if something had been warning him, too late.

The small boat's lead splashed over the side.

'Three fathoms, sir!' A pause. 'Sandy bottom!'

Egmont said nothing, and Bolitho called, *'Oars!'*

The blades halted like stilled wings and the boat idled ahead, the men staring aft at the two uniforms by the tiller.

It was even darker here, more like sunset than afternoon. Just shadow, cloud, land and sea like a wasteland, a heaving desert.

Bolitho tensed and leaned forward, one hand to his ear.

Egmont snapped, 'What is it?'

How many times? How many shores? He felt the stroke oarsman watching him, both hands gripping his loom.

The gentle, regular surge of water on the sand.

He said, 'Give way together! Easy all!' Then, to Egmont, 'The beach, sir.'

And now the land was real, a fine crescent of hard, wet sand and a tangled mass of trees, almost black in this dull light. Like Verling's chart and the scribbled notes he had gathered from somewhere.

'*One* fathom, sir!'

Bolitho felt his mouth go dry.

'Oars! Stand by to beach!'

The sound of the water was louder, and he could see bright phosphorescence streaming from the blades as they glided silently into the shallows.

Then men were leaping over the sides, to control the hull as it ground onto the hard, packed sand; others were running up the beach toward the trees, one of them dropping onto his knee, a musket to his shoulder.

No shouted challenge, or sudden crash of gunfire: the sounds of failure, and of death.

Only the lap of water against the boat's stranded hull, and the hiss of a breeze through the leafless trees.

To himself, Bolitho murmured, 'We did it, Martyn!'

To Egmont he said, 'Shall we cover the boat, sir?'

'Not yet. We don't know if . . .' He appeared to be staring down the beach, beyond the grounded boat, as if he expected to see *Hotspur*. But there was only darkness.

Then he seemed to come out of his trance and said, almost brusquely, 'We must get into position on the ridge, if there proves to *be* one. We will be able to see across the bay.' He stared at Bolitho. 'Well?'

'We could send scouts on ahead, sir. Tinker picked out some good ones. Fair marksmen, too.'

Egmont said, 'It won't come to that, for God's sake. We've got twelve seamen, not a troop of marines!'

He eased his pistol against his hip, marshalling his thoughts.

'We'll move off now. Those scouts – fetch them. And I want the boat shifted nearer the trees, and properly hidden.' He called after him, 'And check those supplies!' He kicked irritably at the sand. 'I can't do everything!'

The trees seemed to move out and around them, the seamen keeping abreast of Bolitho as he trod on firmer ground, the sounds of water on the beach already fading. The thrust and tramp of bodies and the occasional clink of weapons seemed deafening, but he knew it was only imagination. Maybe they were keeping too close together, the habit of sailors thrown ashore, away from their crowded element. It was their way.

He thought of the brief confrontation aboard the flagship. A lifetime ago . . . And the sudden reality of that word. *Trust.*

He quickened his pace and sensed the others following suit on either side of him. Right or wrong, they were with him.

8

Lifeline

'This is far enough. We'll stop while we get our bearings.'
The lieutenant stood by a fallen tree, the pattern of his
buttons oddly bright in the gloom. Bolitho remembered the
corpses he had seen trapped in the submerged wreckage. A
chilling reminder.

Egmont added tartly, 'And keep them quiet! They're like
a herd of damned cattle!'

Bolitho looked at the sky, the clouds moving steadily but
more slowly now, and closer at this height above the sea, on
the crest of the ridge or nearly so. He wanted to stamp his
feet, which were like ice despite the long tramp over rough
ground, uphill for most of the way since they had hidden the
boat. And so quiet, not even the murmur of surf any more,
only wind and the rustle of dead leaves, the clink of metal or
a muttered curse from one of the stooping shadows.

He realised that Egmont was close beside him, could see the oval of his face, hear his breathing. Calm enough, giving nothing away.

He said, 'It will be steeper on the far side. It leads right down to the bay.' He was brushing the front of his coat with one hand as he spoke; a few dead, dry twigs clung to it. It was like seeing him for the first time; he had always been so smart, not a thread or clip out of place. Because he was so new to the rank, or because he still needed to prove something? So different from the unexpected outbursts of anger, or the hostility he had displayed in the cabin. When he had struck Sewell in the face.

'You told me you've detailed two hands as scouts? Can you vouch for them?'

'Keveth and Hooker, sir. When the names were selected. . . .'

Egmont snapped, 'Never mind what Tinker Thorne said. What do *you* think?'

Bolitho pressed his knuckles against his side to control his irritation.

'I'd trust them, sir. Hooker was brought up in the country, and Keveth too, before he volunteered.'

Egmont might have been smiling.

'And he *is* a fellow Cornishman, I believe? Say no more.' He moved to the edge of the rough track, looking back toward the sea. 'We shall make our way down to the bay shortly. Those two men will scout ahead. Don't ask them, Bolitho. *Tell* them. This may be a waste of time, but it may not, and I'll not have any slackness, is that clear?'

Bolitho swung round as several voices let out a collective gasp of surprise or dismay.

Just one light had appeared, moving against the black curtain of sea and sky. Tiny, a mere pinprick, but after the stealth and scent of danger it seemed like a beacon.

Egmont said, 'Hold your noise!' He was feeling his pocket, as if for his watch. '*Hotspur's* riding light. To show others that we are here upon our lawful occasions, if anyone else is fool enough to be abroad at this time!'

Someone muttered, 'The 'ole bloody world'll know by now!'

Egmont moved away from the edge. 'And take that man's name! Any more insolence and I'll see the culprit's backbones at the gangway when we rejoin *Gorgon*!'

Bolitho followed him along the track. They were on the downward slope, and he thought he could feel the sea's nearness, the protection of the little bay he had seen on the chart. When he glanced back, the tiny light had vanished, masked by the fold of the ridge. Like having a line severed, the last link with the small, personal existence they had come to know. And depend on . . . a sailor's faith in his ship.

Egmont was saying, 'Watch your weapons! Keep them covered!'

Keveth, the keen-eyed foretopman who had begun life as a poacher, murmured, 'Ready when you are, sir.'

The second man, Hooker, one of *Gorgon*'s gun captains, raised his fist.

'We won't move too fast for you, sir!'

Bolitho could see his teeth in the darkness. As if he was sharing some private joke, reassuring him of something.

They walked a few yards and they were completely alone.

Keveth turned and said softly, 'Just *us*, see?' He drew a finger across his throat. 'Anyone else gets this!'

How long, how far, Bolitho lost count. He heard the sea, a slow and heavy rhythm like breathing, and the faint ripple of water running over rocks.

Keveth said, 'Bill Hooker's gone off to smell 'un out. Good lad.'

Bolitho forced each muscle to relax. Two Cornishmen on this godforsaken piece of coast, which even now was so hauntingly reminiscent of home. If Keveth took it into his head to leave him, he could simply melt away.

'I bin thinkin', sir. When you gets your new ship. . . .' Keveth was still beside him.

Bolitho smiled. 'I haven't got one yet.'

'Ah, but when ee do. . . .' He broke off, his hand sliding through some wet gorse like a snake. *'Still!'*

But it was Hooker, bent double, grinning when he knew he had found them.

Keveth said, 'Thought ee'd swum back to the ship, my son!'

Bolitho had seen the glint of the dagger before he slipped it back under his coat.

Hooker took a deep breath and slumped down on the ground.

'I *seen* 'er, sir!' He nodded, as if to convince himself as well. 'I got down to the beach. There was a rift in the clouds, an' there she was!'

Keveth exclaimed, 'Bloody saphead! Some 'un might have seen ee!'

'Thought they 'ad. Two of 'em almost trod on me!' He laughed shakily. 'Near thing!'

Bolitho reached over and gripped his arm. He could feel him shivering.

'Tell it as it happened. What you saw, maybe heard. Then we'll go back and tell the others.' He waited, allowing his breathing to slow, and said, 'You did well. I'll see that it's not forgotten.'

Keveth murmured, 'He *will*, too, Bill.'

'I kept close to them rocks, just like you said.' He was looking at his friend, but speaking to Bolitho. 'It was as black as a well, an' then there was a break in the clouds to the nor' west – even saw a few early stars. Then it was gone.'

Bolitho was aware of Keveth's irritation.

'What sort of vessel is she? Square-rigged, fore and aft? Take your time.'

It was hard to remain calm, contained, but any sign of impatience or doubt and Hooker's recollections would be scattered. He thought of Egmont back there in the darkness, doubtless fuming with frustration and cursing Verling for sending him out on this pointless quest. *A waste of time.* What Hooker had to say now would change everything.

Hooker said deliberately, ' 'Tis a brig. I'd swear to that, sir. All canvas furled an' snugged down for the night, I'd say. But she's anchored so far out, it was 'ard to be sure.'

Keveth nudged him.

'Keep goin', Bill. You're doin' handsome.'

Hooker did not seem to hear him. He continued in the same unemotional tone, reliving it. Feeling the menace, alone on the beach.

'There were two boats on the sand, another one moored farther out, in the shallows. Bigger'n the others, one mast, sail-rigged.' He banged the ground with his hand. 'Lee-boards, I'm almost sure.' Another nod to himself. 'Small coaster, I reckon.'

Just the kind of vessel for a dangerous rendezvous. And there would be hundreds of such craft around the islands or used for trade along the French coast.

Hooker continued, 'They was arguin', do you see, sir? Shoutin' some o' the time. I thought they was near comin' to fists or worse.'

Keveth prompted, almost gently, 'English?'

Hooker stared at him, as if it had not occurred to him. 'Some was. Others could 'ave bin French. I ain't sure. But the ones with the coaster was cursin' the crew from the brig. Anchored too far out, one was yellin'.'

Bolitho got to his feet. That had to be the key. *Too far out.* Whatever was being unlawfully traded or moved to another rendezvous, and was worth cold-blooded murder, had to be shifted *now.*

He said, 'Hazardous or not, they have no choice.' He thought of *Hotspur*'s isolated riding light. Neither did Verling.

He looked at Keveth, who was also standing now, his carefully wrapped musket over one shoulder.

'I'll have you relieved as soon as I can. We'll go and find the others.'

Keveth hesitated, as if some sharp comment was hanging on his tongue. But he said, 'I'll be here, sir. The lieutenant will be wantin' a boat's crew, I'm thinkin'.' He added firmly, 'I'd like to keep with you,' and wiped his grubby chin with the back of his hand. *'Sir!'*

It was only a short time before they found the others, but long enough for the truth to become clear to him.

A boat's crew was needed without delay. Verling must have known it even as he was grappling with each doubt. If he had waited until dawn, the mystery ship would have sailed, despite the risks in these shoal-ridden waters. The alternative was the end of a rope.

And the smuggled cargo which had reached this far?

He recalled Dancer's quiet speculation. It was certainly neither rum nor tea.

Egmont waited for Bolitho to stride up to him.

'Well?'

Impatient, anxious, even excited? For once, he was hiding his emotions.

'Hooker has had a quick sighting, sir. A brig, anchored well out.'

Egmont glanced at the seaman in question.

'Anything else? Got a tongue, has he?'

Hooker swallowed hard.

'There was men on the beach, boats as well.' When

Egmont failed to interrupt he continued in his round country accent, but there was nothing slow-witted about his observations. Bolitho had watched him at numerous drills aboard *Gorgon*, as gun captain of one of her long eighteen-pounders; his brain was fast enough.

Egmont waited in that enigmatic silence, and then said, 'Some were French, you think?'

Hooker shrugged. 'I thought they was, sir.'

Egmont looked at the sky. 'Probably locals. They speak a Norman-French patois here. No better breeding ground for smuggling on the grand scale.' He broke off, as if surprised at himself for sharing his opinions. He regarded Bolitho coldly. 'If the vessel is anchored far out, and it seems wise in these waters, that will mean they must begin loading their contraband straight away. No time to lose. Two boats, you say?'

Hooker spread his hands. 'An' the coaster.'

Egmont folded and unfolded his arms. 'The brig would have one, maybe two more. All the same. . . .'

Bolitho said, 'A long haul, even so.'

Egmont stared past him, watching or listening to the trees.

'Wind's livelier. They might not have noticed that aboard *Hotspur*. More sheltered beyond the point.'

Bolitho said, 'Mr. Verling will have given strict orders. . . .' He got no further.

'I know that, damn it! But he won't have any idea of the timing needed. *I* shall deal with that immediately.' He swung round and looked at the huddle of dark shapes, crouching on the cold ground or in the shelter of a few salt-bitten trees. 'I want a boat's crew *now*. Hooker, you lead the way. You can tell Mr. Verling what you told me.' He checked him with his hand. 'And make sure you get it right, man! It will be upon your head!'

Bolitho felt the anger churning at his guts. No word of praise or thanks, only a threat of recrimination. He recalled Keveth's words. *I'd like to keep with you.* He had already guessed, known, that Egmont would be returning to *Hotspur* with a boat's crew. In the shortest possible time. It made sense. And yet. . . .

Egmont was looking at the sky again. 'Take charge until you receive further orders. Observe their movements, but remain out of sight.' He turned away. 'Select five hands to stay with you. I shall manage with the other half of the party.'

Someone muttered, 'Done, sir. I've picked our lads.'

Bolitho forced himself to concentrate, to blot out the glaring truth. He was being left behind, with only five of the original landing party. Keveth had known; so, probably, had Hooker.

The voice at his elbow was that of Price, the big Welshman who had been the boat's leadsman on their passage to the beach. He was known for a rough and irrepressible sense of humour, not always appreciated by Tinker, the boatswain's mate.

'That's long enough!' Egmont was watching the small group of figures breaking up, separating into two sections, a few grins and remarks here, a quick pat on a friend's shoulder there.

Hooker paused for the merest second by Bolitho.

'I'll pass the word to Mr. Dancer, sir.' That was all. It was enough.

Egmont's people were already moving back beneath the trees at the foot of the ridge. In two hours he would be in the boat; in three or thereabouts, in *Hotspur*'s cabin.

He left without a backward look. Was that how it had to be?

Will I be expected to behave like that when – if – my chance comes?

Price was still beside him. 'Well, there you are, see. The cream always comes out on top!' One of the others even laughed.

Bolitho said, 'Let's find a scrap of cover – I think I felt more rain. This is what we'll do.'

For an instant he believed he had imagined it.

But he had not. He was in charge. And he was ready.

9

In the King's Name

Richard Bolitho pressed down on both hands to take the
weight of his body and ease the pain in his legs. He was
wedged between two great shoulders of rock, worn smooth
by the sea. He could hear the slap and sluice of trapped
water somewhere below his precarious perch, like a
warning, sharpening his mind. The tide was on the make,
or soon would be. That would mean climbing higher,
losing contact, or worse, any protection he and his small
party had gained.

He leaned forward once more. He had lost count of how
many times he had repeated the movement, staring at the
faint curve of the beach and the ungainly outline of the
lugger Hooker had described, more at an angle now,
pulling restlessly at the anchor which prevented her from
grinding onto this treacherous shore.

He closed his eyes and tried to focus his thoughts. At first, when Keveth had guided him to this point, he had feared immediate discovery. Every loose pebble, or the splash of feet across wet sand, had sounded like a landslide, *a herd of cattle* as Egmont had so contemptuously called them. But the dark, scrambling figures, the occasional shouts of instruction or anger across the water had continued uninterrupted. The two longboats had been loaded and had pulled strongly away from the beach. It would take several journeys to complete the transfer of the lugger's cargo. It had probably been their original intention to moor directly alongside. *Too far out.*

It was that important even now. Important enough to kill for.

He tensed as sand splashed into the water below him, and realised that the curved hanger was already partly drawn, the hilt cold in his fist. But it was Keveth, and he had not even seen him until he was here, only an arm's length away.

Keveth had turned and was looking down toward the beach.

Then he said, 'One of the boats is comin' back now.' He was breathing evenly, apparently at ease. 'Next load'll be ready to move directly. Heavy work, no doubt o' that!'

Bolitho heard the creak of oars; men jumping from the boat to guide it into the shallows, somebody barking an order. It could have been any language.

'Did you see what they're carrying?'

Keveth was watching him; he could almost feel his eyes.

'Guns.' He was peering at the beach again. 'I knew 'twas summat heavy. I seen muskets stowed like that afore.' He let his words sink in. 'New ones, anyway.'

Bolitho stared into the darkness; the blood seemed to be pounding in his ears like the sea beyond these rocks. No wonder the prize was worth the risk. Worth human life.

And yet there must be houses, perhaps farms quite close by. . . .

Keveth must have read his thoughts.

'Well, ee d' know what 'tis like at home. Nobody sees nowt when th' Brotherhood is out.'

But all Bolitho could think of was the shipment of guns. Where bound? And destined for whose hands?

There had been rumours. The more radical news-sheets had openly used the word 'rebellion' in the American colonies ever since the Boston Massacre. And only days ago one of the lieutenants in *Gorgon* had claimed it was the subject of the admiral's conference. Even Captain Conway had mentioned it.

It had seemed so distant, so vague. Another quarterdeck whisper. But if true . . . just across the water, the old enemy would be quick to encourage any such insurrection.

Keveth was on his knees, peering once more at the beach.

''Nother boat comin' in. Must be a load o' muskets. Th' lugger's leeboards is well above th' line.'

Bolitho glanced up at the sky. Hooker had seen the first stars. There were more now, and the torn clouds seemed to have gathered speed. He thought of *Hotspur*'s riding light, unreachable beyond the ridge. And of Egmont, brushing dead leaves from his coat. He had once heard someone remark that Egmont's father was, or had been, a tailor at one of the naval ports. That might explain. . . .

He pushed it away and said, 'It's up to us.' He tried to shut out the other voice. *It's up to you.* 'The tide's on the make. They'll be weighing anchor before we know it.'

Keveth said, 'I dunno much about such things, but us Jacks ain't supposed to. Rebellion or freedom, *we* obey orders an' that's all there is to it. It's which end of the gun you're standin' at that counts in th' end!'

Bolitho stood up suddenly to prevent himself from changing his mind, one hand against the rock to take his weight. He could feel his heart thudding against his ribs.

'I must get nearer.' He thought Keveth would protest. Now, while there was still time. He was outspoken enough; he had proved that. Sharp and clear, like a lookout's view from the topsail yard. Five seamen, who could just as easily turn their backs as obey a direct command that might end in death. And who would know? Or care?

Keveth looked at him in silence, and Bolitho thought he had not heard. Then he moved swiftly, reaching out toward his face, as if to strike him. But he was touching one of the white patches on Bolitho's lapel. 'Better hide them middy's patches. Stand out like a priest in a brothel.' He folded the collar deftly. 'Best be goin', then.'

Bolitho felt him grasp his elbow as they descended from the rocks: unreal, and strangely moving. And not once had he called him *sir*. Which made it even stronger, because it mattered.

Perhaps this was madness, and it was already too late.

But through it all he could hear Martyn's voice, just before he had climbed down into the boat and cast off from *Hotspur*'s side, a thousand years ago. . . .

Glory can wait. Until I'm with you.

He said, 'You *are*.' Then he joined the seaman who had once been a poacher, and together they stared at the pale, coffin-like shapes which had been hauled onto the sand.

Even in the shelter of the rocks, he could feel the increasing thrust of the wind. A long, hard pull for the men in the boats, even with extra hands.

Keveth pointed. ''Nother box.'

Bolitho saw the shape being lowered over the side of the lugger, heard the squeak of block and tackle and the louder splashes of men wading through icy water with the next load of muskets. No shouts or curses this time. They were probably breathless.

He asked, 'How many hands still aboard, d'you think?'

'Three or four. Enough for th' winch, watchin th' anchor cable as well. If that parted. . . .'

He ducked as someone shouted, but nothing else happened. The box had been manhandled further along the beach and onto firmer sand. The would have the wind against them all the way back when they came for the next load.

Bolitho pushed the hair from his eyes. The last one, perhaps.

He said, 'Might be the time to act.' He recalled Egmont's words when they had landed. *Don't ask them. Tell them!*

He tried to gauge the distance from the rocks to the moored lugger. They would have to wade through the water, farther than they thought. He knew he was deluding himself. The tide was already coming in, noisier now with the wind in its face.

'When the other boat shoves off . . .' He touched Keveth's arm. It did not flinch. 'We'll board her.'

He saw another pale shape jerking slowly down the side close to the leeboard. Hooker would have described all this to Verling. What would the first lieutenant be thinking? If he had listened to Egmont, *Hotspur* would be snugged down in St. Peter Port by now, and somebody else would be responsible, reaping the praise or the blame.

Bolitho considered the others in this small party. Price was a steady, reliable hand, in spite of the humour so often aimed at his superiors. The other three he knew only by sight, and in the daily routine, and in the past few weeks he had not seen much of that. He thought of his brother Hugh, in temporary command of the revenue cutter *Avenger*. A stranger. And yet Dancer had spent a lot of time with him. Getting on well together, it had seemed.

Don't ask them. Tell them. Even that sounded like Hugh.

He said, 'Are you with me?'

Keveth did not answer directly, but turned to listen as the second boat was pushed and manhandled into the water. Then he unslung the carefully wrapped musket from his shoulder and said, 'Work for old Tom 'ere, after all!'

He faced the midshipman again. 'All the way, *sir.*'
It was time.

Bolitho was aware of the others pressing around him, could feel their breathing and, perhaps, their doubts.

'We'll board her now, before the boats come back. This wind will carry us out. After that we can stand clear and wait for *Hotspur.*'

'Suppose the tide gets other ideas, sir?'

Bolitho put a face to the voice. Perry, an experienced seaman who had been with him when they had found the dead boat's crew. Tough, withdrawn. But observant. If the wind dropped, the lugger would run hard aground as soon as the cable was cut.

Price said, 'I've seen boats like this one before, sir. No keel to speak of – they use the leeboards if they need steerage way. Used to watch the Dutchmen when I was over on the Medway and they came across the Channel.'

Another voice. His name was Stiles. Younger, and aggressive, said to have been a bare-knuckle prizefighter around the markets until he had decided to sign on. In a hurry, it was suggested.

'Will there be a reward?'

Bolitho felt the winter wind in his face, wet sand stinging the skin. At any moment the chance might desert them. At best they might be able to drift clear of the shore until *Hotspur* up-anchored and made an appearance. The lugger would provide enough evidence for any future action.

He said bluntly, 'It's our duty!' and almost expected the man to laugh.

Instead, Stiles replied, 'That'll 'ave to do, then!'

The remaining seaman was named Drury, a sure-footed topman like Keveth. He had been flogged for insolence, and Bolitho had seen the old scars on his back once when he had been working in the shrouds aboard *Gorgon*. Curiously, he had been among the first hands selected by Tinker for the passage crew. As boatswain's mate, Tinker himself had probably dealt out the punishment.

Drury said thoughtfully, 'Might get a tot o' somethin' to warm our guts if we make a move right now!'

Bolitho felt someone nudge him. It was Keveth.

'See, sir? They'm good as gold when you puts it like that.'

Bolitho faced the sea and tried not to hear the hiss of spray along the beach. Then it was surging around his legs, dragging at him like some human force as he strode toward the lugger.

They would fall back, leave him to die because of his own stupid determination. And for what?

It was like a wild dream, the icy sea dragging at his body, and surging past the lugger which seemed to be shining despite the darkness, mocking him.

He slipped and would have been dragged down by the current, out of his depth, but for a hand gripping his shoulder. The fingers were like iron, forcing him forward. And suddenly, the blunt hull was leaning directly over him, the pale outline of the leeboard just as Hooker had described it, and the loose hoisting tackle dragging against him, caught on the incoming crests. Like those other times, in training or in deadly earnest, he was scrambling up the side, using the hard, wet tackle and kicking every foot of the way. He felt metal scrape his thigh like a knife edge, and almost cried out with shock and disbelief as he lurched to his feet. He was on the lugger's deck.

'Cut the cable!'

But the cry of the wind and the surge of water alongside seemed to muffle his voice. Then he heard a thud, and another, someone yelling curses, and knew it was Price's boarding axe taking a second swing.

He felt the deck shudder and for an instant thought they had run ashore. But the hull was steady, and somehow he knew it was moving, free from the ground.

A figure seemed to rise from the very deck, arms waving, mouth a black hole in his face. Yelling, screaming, unreal.

And then a familiar voice, harsh but steady. 'Oh, no, you don't, matey!'

And the sickening crack of a heavy blade into bone.

Bolitho gasped, 'Fores'l!' But he should have recognised the confusion of wet canvas, already breaking into life.

He staggered across the deck, toward a solitary figure grappling with the long tiller-bar. It was Drury, with a cutlass thrust through his belt.

'Steady she is, sir!' He laughed into the wind. 'Almost!'

There was a small hatch, and Bolitho saw that he had nearly fallen into it. Two more figures were crouched on a ladder, shouting; perhaps they were pleading. Only then did he realise that the hanger was in his hand, and the blade was only a foot away from the nearest man.

He yelled, 'You two, bear a hand! *Now*, damn you!'

His words might have been lost in the noise of wind and flapping canvas, but the naked blade was clear in any language.

Price was calling, 'She's answering, sir! We'll tackle the mains'l now!'

Bolitho stared at the sky, and saw the big foresail swaying above him like a shadow.

'Are we all here?' He wanted to laugh or weep. Like madness.

Keveth shouted, 'Large as life, sir!'

There was a muffled splash and he added. 'That 'un won't bother us no more!'

Bolitho tried to sheathe the hanger in its scabbard, but felt Keveth take it gently from his hand.

'Don't need this for a bit, sir.' He was grinning. 'We've taken th' old girl!'

Bolitho moved to the side and stared at the choppy wavelets below him. He was shaking badly, and not because of the cold. Or the danger. And it was hard to think, and make sense of it. They would winch up the mainsail and steer a course clear of this rocky coastline.

At first light . . . But nothing would form clearly in his mind, except, *we did it*.

Below deck they might find more muskets, evidence which would justify *Hotspur*'s actions.

And ours.

Tomorrow . . . He looked at the stars. He was no longer shivering. And it was tomorrow now.

He heard someone else, 'Too bloody late, you bastards!' and the immediate crack of a musket. But even that was distorted by the wind and rigging.

Then Keveth, sharp, angry, 'Get under cover an' reload *now*, you mad bugger! You'll 'ave a dead charge on your 'ands with the next shot!'

There were shouts and another shot and Bolitho remembered that the boats were out there, lost in the swell as they pulled toward the beach. Another few minutes and they would have foiled any attempt to board the lugger, and there would be corpses rolling in the tide to mark their folly. He ran to the side and peered past the tiller. It was not imagination. He could see the vague outline of the ridge, edged against the sky, where before there had been solid blackness. Clouds, too, but the stars had gone.

Keveth called, 'That'll show the bastards!' But he was staring after the one who had fired his musket. 'They'll be comin' for us – they've nowhere else to turn to!' He waved his fist to drive the point home. 'Listen!'

The rattle and creak of loose gear seemed to fade, and in a lull in the wind Bolitho could hear the slow, regular *clink, clink, clink*, like that last time, when they had left Plymouth. The pawls of a capstan, men straining every muscle against wind and tide to break out the anchor. The brig was making a run for it. Those in the boats, even their own hands, were being abandoned. There were no rules for the smuggling fraternity but *save your own neck first.* He banged his fist on the bulwark, the pain steadying him.

The brutal truth was that *Hotspur* might still be at anchor, unwilling to risk any dangerous manoeuvre on the mere chance of an encounter. He recalled Verling's parting words. *No heroics.*

He joined Drury by the tiller-bar and leaned his weight against it. He could feel the heavy shudder, the power of the sea, and tried to guess at their progress. Without more sail and time to work clear of the bay . . . He shut his mind to the ifs and the maybes. They had done better than anyone could have expected. Hoped.

'The brig's weighed, sir!' Another voice said, 'Cut 'er cable, more like!'

Either way, the smuggler was making sail. If she worked around *Hotspur* or avoided her altogether, her master would have the open sea ahead, and every point of the compass from which to choose his escape.

And even if there was further evidence below deck, what would that prove? The two cowering wretches who had pleaded for mercy when Keveth and his mates had swarmed aboard would certainly go to the gallows, or hang in chains on the outskirts of some seaport or along a coastal road as a grisly warning to others. But the trade would never stop while men had gold to offer. Personal greed or to sustain a rebellion, the cause mattered little to those who were prepared to take the risk for profit.

He heard a cry from forward: Stiles, the prizefighter, poised high in the bows, one arm flung out.

Bolitho wiped his face. It was not a trick of light or imagination. He could see the young seaman outlined against the heaving water and occasional feather of spray, and then, reaching out on either side, an endless, pale backdrop of sea and sky.

Then he heard Stiles' voice. Clear and sharp. *'Breakers ahead!'*

'Helm a-lee!' He saw the tiller going over, one of the captured smugglers running to throw his weight with Drury's to bring it round.

Bolitho saw Keveth staring at him, as if telling him something, but all he could think was that he could see each feature, and that he still had his musket, 'old Tom', across one shoulder. As if all time had stopped, and only here and this moment counted for anything.

Stiles was stepping down from his perch in the bows, still watching the sea and the lazy turmoil of breakers. Not a reef, and at high water it would be little more than shallows. A sandbar. But enough.

And here too was the brig, her courses and foretopsail already set and filling to the wind, even a small, curling wave at her stem. Moving through the grey water, her hull still in darkness. Like an onlooker. Uninvolved.

'Pass the word! Stand by to ram!'

It could have been someone else's voice.

More of a sensation than a shock, the most noise coming from the flapping canvas as the handful of seamen ran to slacken off all lines and free the winch.

They had ground ashore, with hardly a shudder. When

the tide turned again she would be high and dry.

Bolitho walked aft and watched the brig, heeling slightly as she altered course, her sails hardening, a masthead pendant whipping out like a spear.

The seaman named Perry shook his fist.

'We did our best, damn their eyes!'

'Not enough. . . .' Bolitho flinched as someone gripped his arm. *'What?'* And saw Keveth's expression. Not shock or surprise, but the face of a man who could no longer be caught aback by anything.

He said quietly, 'An' *there's* a sight, sir. One you'll long remember.'

It was *Hotspur*, lying over to the wind, casting her own shadow like a reflection across the whitecaps. She had skirted the headland, so closely that she appeared to be balanced across it.

Keveth swung round. 'Wait, sir! What're you about?' He was staring up at him as Bolitho ran to the side and climbed into the shrouds.

'So that he'll know!' He was unfolding the collar of his coat, until the white midshipman's patches were clearly visible. 'Give me my hat!'

He reached down and took it without losing sight of the brig. Verling would see him, and know what they had done. That this fight had not been so one-sided after all. That his trust had not been misplaced.

But who did he really mean? *So that he'll know. . . .*

'Boat! Larboard quarter!'

Price turned away. 'Easy, Ted! It's our lads!'

118

He looked up at the midshipman in the shrouds, one hand holding his hat steady against the wind. To others, it might look like a salute. They would not see his torn and stained uniform across the water. But they would see him. And they would not forget.

Bolitho heard none of it, watching the two sets of sails. On a converging tack, the land rolling back like a screen. There was light on the water now, a faint margin between sea and sky, but hardly visible. Or real.

Hotspur made a fine sight, *the bird unfolding her wings*. Ready to attack.

Too far away to see any movement, but he could hold the image clearly in his mind. Swivel guns manned, puny but deadly at close quarters. *Hotspur*'s two bow-chasers would be empty, useless. Someone would answer for that. Later, perhaps, when they read Verling's log. Written in Martyn's familiar hand.

And bright patches of scarlet as if painted on a canvas: Verling had hoisted two ensigns, so that there could be no mistake or excuse. *Hotspur* had become a man-of-war.

He heard the boat come alongside, voices, excited greetings. Then silence as they all turned to watch the two vessels, almost overlapping, *Hotspur* graceful, even fragile, against her adversary.

There was anger now, alarm too, at the far-off sounds of shots, like someone tapping casually on a tabletop with his fingers.

Hotspur must have misjudged her change of tack, as if, out of control, she would drive her jib boom through the brig's foremast shrouds. But she had luffed, and must surely be almost abeam. Then there was a brief, vivid flash, and seconds later the sharp, resonant bang of a swivel gun.

The seamen around him were suddenly quiet, each man in his mind across the grey water with his friend or companion, and at his proper station. This was like being rendered helpless, cut off from the only world they knew.

Keveth said, 'What the *hell*! If only. . . .'

The two vessels were still drifting together, sails in disarray, as if no human hands were at the helm of either.

There was a great gasp, mounting to a combined growl, like something torn from each man's heart. Just a small sliver of scarlet, but it was moving slowly up the brig's overlapping mainyard, and then it broke out to the wind. To match the two flags flying from *Hotspur*'s masts.

Bolitho could not tear his eyes away, despite the wild burst of cheering, and the hard slaps across his shoulders.

'That showed 'em!' and 'That made the murderin' buggers jump!'

One seaman, the boat's coxswain, was trying to make himself heard.

'I'm to take you aboard, sir! Mr. Verling's orders!'

Bolitho seized Keveth's arm and said, 'You're in charge, until they send someone to relieve you.' He shook him gently. 'I'll not forget what you did. Believe me.' He walked after the boat's coxswain, but paused and looked back at his own small party of sailors. Price, the big Welshman; even he was at a loss for a joke now. Perry,

Stiles, and Drury, who was still standing by the stiff and motionless tiller-bar, his face split by one huge grin.

Then he was in the boat, faster and lighter now without the weight of extra hands sent by Verling. Rising and plunging across each rank of incoming waves, and all the time the tall pyramids of sails seemed to draw no closer. Only once did he turn to gaze back at the beached lugger, and the small cluster of figures by the stern.

'Stand by, bowman!'

He hardly remembered going alongside, only hands reaching out and down to assist him aboard: familiar faces, but all like strangers. He wanted to shake himself, be carried by this moment and its triumph and thrust the strain or uncertainty, or was it fear, into the retreating shadows.

He could still feel their hands pounding his shoulders, see their grins, and Keveth's pride and satisfaction. The victors.

He stared around, and across to the other vessel's poop. The wheel was in fragments, the bulwark pitted and broken by the single blast of canister from *Hotspur*'s swivel. There was blood, too, and he could hear someone groaning in agony, and another quietly sobbing.

He saw Egmont, back turned, his drawn sword across his shoulder, quite still, as if on parade.

'This way, sir!' A seaman touched his arm.

He saw some of them pause to glance at him, and young Sewell, his rough bandage still dangling from one leg. Staring, raising his hand to acknowledge him, his face changed in some way. Older. . . .

Verling was by the compass box, hatless, and without a sword.

'You did damned well,' he said.

But Bolitho could not speak, or move. As if everything had stopped. Like the moment when the scarlet ensign had appeared above the brig's deck.

He saw that Verling had a bandage around his wrist, and here, also, there was blood. Beyond him, splinters had been torn from the deck. Like feathers, where those few shots had left their mark.

Verling said, 'If there was any way. . . .' He broke off, and gestured abruptly at the hatch. 'He's in the cabin. We did all. . . .'

Bolitho did not hear the rest.

He was down the ladder and in the cabin, where they had sat and waited. Talked about the Board and the future.

Dancer was on one of the bench seats, his head and shoulders propped on some cushions. He had been watching the door, perhaps listening. Now he tried to reach out, but his arm fell to his side.

There was one lamp burning in the cabin, near the same skylight beneath which Verling had been standing during that final discussion. The light was moving unsteadily as the hull nudged against the captive vessel alongside, and gave colour to Dancer's fair hair, but revealed the pallor of his skin and the effort of his breathing. There was a small red stain on his shirt.

Bolitho took his hand and held it between his own, and watched his eyes, trying to keep the pain at bay, or to experience it himself. Like all those other times.

'I came as soon as I could, Martyn. I didn't know. . . .'
He felt the hand move in his, attempting to return his grip.

He said, 'You're here now, Dick. All that matters.'

Bolitho leaned over him, shielding his face, his eyes,
from the light. He could barely hear the words.

The hand moved again. Then, just one word. 'Together.'

Someone spoke. Bolitho had not known there was
anybody else in the cabin. It was Tinker.

'Best leave him, sir. He's gone, I'm afraid.'

Bolitho touched his friend's face, gently, to wipe away
some tears. The skin was quite still. And he realised the
tears were his own.

Somewhere, in another world, he heard the trill of a
boatswain's call, the response of running feet.

Tinker was by the door, blocking it. In his years at sea he
had seen and done almost everything. In ships as different
as the oceans they served, and with captains just as varied.
You became hardened to most things. Or you went under.

He had heard the new activity on deck. He was needed
now, more than ever. The prisoners to be put to work, both
vessels to be got under way again. Maybe a jury-rig to be
fitted aboard the brig's steering as the helm had been shot
away. The first lieutenant had no doubt been yelling for
him already.

But it was the here and now that required him most.

'Listen, me son. Soon, maybe very soon, you'll be
standin' into a new life. You have their respect, I've seen
you win it, but that's only the beginning. You'll make

friends, an' you'll lose some of 'em. Sure, that's the way of it. It's a sailor's lot.'

The calls were silent, the feet on deck were still. The hard, leathery hand touched his torn sleeve very briefly.

'Just think of the next watch, an' the next horizon, see?'

Bolitho turned by the door and glanced back. He could be asleep. Waiting for the next watch.

He felt his lips move and heard himself speak, and the words were dry and controlled, and the voice unfamiliar.

'I'm ready. When you are.' He looked at the door again. 'You'll never know.'

The way ahead. *Together.*

Epilogue

Captain Beves Conway swung away from the stern windows of his day cabin and called, 'Have him come aft directly, man!'

He had been watching the thirty-two gun frigate *Condor* enter harbour and drop anchor with a minimum of fuss and delay; it was what he would expect from a captain like Maude. Always busy, always in demand. He cocked his head to listen to his own ship's routine, and almost sighed with relief. The disruption of overhaul was finished, until their lordships insisted on another; the constant comings and goings of working parties and dockyard experts and the noise, smells and personal discomfort were being inflicted on some other vessel, and His Britannic Majesty's Ship *Gorgon* could now show even a frigate a thing or two if required. Freshly blackened standing rigging and gleaming paintwork were shining brightly, despite a morning so cold and misty that even the usually restless gulls seemed content to float upon the anchorage like discarded wreaths.

The screen door opened a few inches, and the lieutenant said, 'Mr. Bolitho, sir. He has apologised for the state of his uniform.' He said it without a smile, unlike Verling. It felt strange to have another officer standing in for him until his return from Guernsey. Verling would be fretting over the delay. He would have heard all the latest news from the colonies when *Condor* had called at St. Peter Port with the admiral's despatches.

It would be good to have him back as first lieutenant. Although he might feel quite differently about it, after his brief but exciting flirtation with the schooner *Hotspur*.

Conway glanced at the letters lying open on his desk; they had been sent across from *Condor* within minutes of her anchor hitting the bottom.

One letter had been from his old friend's son, Midshipman Andrew Sewell. He was still with Verling and the passage crew in Guernsey, but the short, simple note had seemed like a reward, something which had warmed him more than he would have believed, or hoped.

The door opened, and Richard Bolitho walked into the cabin. This was only just February, and much had happened since their last meeting, the Board held in the flagship, which was still moored in exactly the same position as the day when several 'young gentlemen' had been required to face their tormentors. They all had to endure it, and laughed about it afterwards. The fortunate ones, anyway.

He strode to meet him and clasped his hands.

'So good to see you again, my boy! I want to hear all about the capture of the smugglers, and the contraband you helped to seize. It will carry some weight, I can tell you, with their lordships, and above!'

He guided him to a chair and the table where a servant had laid out some wine and his best goblets.

'I arranged for you to take passage in *Condor*. I hope it was a pleasant, if uneventful one?' He did not wait for a reply; he rarely did. 'I know you will have a good deal to do, and I shall not delay you unnecessarily. My clerk will take care of the other matters.'

Bolitho leaned his back against the chair. The same ship; even the weather, cold and grey, had not changed. The houses of Plymouth, like the ranks of anchored ships, were still half-shrouded in mist. It had seemed to take an eternity for the frigate to make her entrance and anchor.

And yet only days had passed since it had begun. When they had climbed aboard *Hotspur*, a lifetime ago.

He glanced down at the breeches someone had loaned him, and at the makeshift patches on his coat. Reminders, like the cuts and bruises on his body.

The captain had poured the wine himself and was smiling down at him.

'I am very proud of you, Richard. One of *my* midshipmen.' He raised his glass. 'No need for you to be delayed when it could be avoided. I had a word with the flag captain.' He was refilling his glass, although Bolitho did not recall tasting the wine. 'And I wanted to do it myself.' He pulled open a drawer and took out an unsealed envelope. 'You are free to leave the ship and complete your arrangements.'

He watched him take the envelope, the 'scrap of parchment' they all joked about. Afterwards.

'Your commission, Richard. None better deserved!'

Bolitho saw his goblet being refilled. And still he could taste nothing.

It was here. The moment, the impossible step. He had seen some of the frigate's midshipmen glancing over at him during their brief time together. All so young, like Sewell . . . although Sewell had seemed suddenly mature.

And his first appointment. *You are herewith directed and commanded, upon receipt of these orders . . .* The rest was blurred.

But it was a frigate, named *Destiny*.

Conway was saying, 'I shall delay you no longer.' He looked over at the desk. 'Young Andrew Sewell has told me what you did for him. It helped him more than you can know. His father would have been obliged to you, had he been here himself to thank you.'

Bolitho stood up; there were voices in the outer cabin. He was grateful for the interruption, and so, possibly, was the captain.

He said, 'Martyn Dancer was a great help to him, sir. They got on well together.'

Conway walked with him to the screen door, and impetuously put his arm around Bolitho's shoulder. Afterwards, the cabin servant remarked that he had never

128

seen Conway do anything like it, and it was never repeated.

Conway said, 'Then my thanks are to you both.' He looked again at the stern windows. 'God be with you when you join *Destiny*,' and he paused. 'As a King's officer.'

Out on the broad quarterdeck the air was still misty, but there was a gleam on the water, as if the sun were about to break through.

He would go to Falmouth and tell his mother and sister. It would have to be a brief visit, and he was glad of that also.

He looked around the familiar decks, and at the groups of seamen and marines.

This was the past. Ahead lay the new horizon.